PRINCESS THE CAT VERSUS SNARL THE COYOTE

A CAT AND DOG ADVENTURE

JOHN HEATON

FLANNEL AND FLASHLIGHT PRESS

Princess the Cat Versus Snarl the Coyote
A Dog and Cat Adventure

Flannel and Flashlight Press
Cissna Park, IL

www.flannelandflashlight.com

―――――

First Print Edition
ISBN: 9781520431871

1

W *hat was that?*

I stand still except for my twitching ears, scanning about my domain. The cool night breeze carries the noise to me again.

It is the sound of disrespect and rebellion.

I hear the *tink tink* from a bell on a collar. I'm sure a foreign cat lurks on the edge of the yard two houses away. The people at that house do an exceedingly poor job of caring for my lawn there, and so I've designated that yard as my toilet.

Is it possible that the people who live there got a cat?

Surely not.

Otherwise, Chief would have told me about it. He's an elderly dog who lives next door. He can hardly move or see. However, he's been here ever since I arrived at my coronation and received my name: *Princess*. He's as respectable as dogs get.

I don't have time to ask Chief now. I move to investigate this invader. Bells on a collar signal disrespect and rebellion because they put me and my kingdom in danger.

Bells on cat collars attract coyotes.

They may scare birds away from the cat, but they also lure in vile coyotes.

I slink to a nearby yard. My dark gray tabby coat makes for excellent stealth maneuvering at night. But I've lost track of the invader now. I wait a second, and its bell gives its position away as it leaps over the back fence into an adjacent yard.

I follow it over the back fence seconds later. I see the invader now. It's a kitten, barely old enough to be out on its own. She's completely white, and her collar is pink. A bell dangles from it. She hasn't spotted me yet, but I have no doubt that this upstart wants to become the new empress.

I do not tolerate rivals.

I track her over fences and through yards and gardens until we are in the neighbor's backyard directly behind my own.

Two things happen at the same time.

This kitten meets up with another kitten who appears to be her twin brother. He has a blue collar with a bell on it, and he is also completely white. I also smell an unmistakable odor, a smell I will never forget. I rush up a tree for a higher vantage point over this new and more dangerous intruder whom the kitten invited into my kingdom.

I smell Snarl. Snarl is the leader of the coyotes.

My first instinct is to let Snarl take these kittens. But I can't allow Snarl, or any coyote for that matter, into my domain. I don't see Snarl, but I do smell him.

I see a coyote enter the yard, but it's not Snarl. Snarl is nearby. I still smell him. I don't know why a different coyote is here. This coyote comes out of the shadows and inches towards the two kittens. The kittens glob together and form a shivering ball of white fur.

As a tandem, they shift away from the coyote and towards the shed. I creep down closer amongst the potted plants along the fence so I can see the action. The interloping coyote must be young and unsure of himself.

Has he never taken a kitten home for his dinner?

The coyote walks directly under one of the potted plants near me. I'm going to push it down on top of him. It should frighten the coyote away and summon people out of the house.

I place my front paws on the pot to push it over, but then I hear the coyote say the most perplexing thing.

"I'm sorry," he stammers. "I don't want to hurt you."

I pause to hear more.

"I'm so sorry. I'll have to take one of you," the coyote continues, "because if I don't, Snarl will kick me out of the pack."

Then, one of the kittens does something even more perplexing. The boy kitten with the blue collar walks up to the coyote. He lowers his head and offers the scruff of his neck.

The coyote leans in with his jaws open to snatch the kitten. I push the pot over the edge before his teeth clamp down on the soft white fur. It crashes onto the concrete, missing narrowly. It startles the coyote, and I leap down onto his back. My claws dig into his flesh, and I *yowl* as loudly as I can. The vile coyote howls and tries to get away. He frees himself with a sharp twist, but only after I inflict deep scratches.

A light in the people's house turns on, and the back door opens. A man person comes out with a broom, ready to strike whatever he sees, but the coyote has fled, and I've already melted into the shadows. He scoops up the trembling kittens, carries them inside and shuts the sliding glass door.

I replay what happened over and over in my mind. A coyote who didn't want to take a weak kitten? A kitten who gave himself up for another?

Baffling.

One thing I know for sure is that Snarl will come soon for vengeance. I smelled him nearby, and that young coyote was surely from his pack.

For now, the owners of these new kittens deserve a lesson for foolishly putting bells on their cats. I sniff around to make sure that all coyotes are indeed gone, and then I climb down the fence. I walk into the light cast through the sliding glass door. Nothing moves or reacts to my presence, and so I walk all the way to their back step. I notice they have a nice mat right outside their back door.

I don't have the urge, but this is the best way to let people know Princess is unhappy. I squat over their doormat and relieve myself.

That should teach them.

That's enough for one night. I head back to my own people's house. Coyotes howl in the distance as I enter my garage through the cat door on its side.

2

L ater the next morning, I'm in that magical place between sleep and consciousness. I know I must be partly awake and not merely dreaming because I feel the sun stream through the window and warm my tummy. I open one of my eyes a sliver and confirm my location. I'm sprawled in the best sunning spot of all my domain. I'm laying on my big people's bed, exactly where the morning sun comes in through the windows. I hear the footsteps of my people's children approaching, and I am certain I am not dreaming.

Children are never in my dreams, except for my scary dreams.

Them and coyotes.

"Hi, Princess!" the youngest girl says inches from my face as she tries to rub my back. I don't like how she blocks my sun. I emit a low growl, hoping she understands I don't like to be touched. She doesn't seem to understand.

"Leave her alone," the boy says coming in after her. "She's a grouchy cat." I appreciate his honesty but detect disrespect in his observation. They back away when my growl crescendos.

"Princess needs friends. At least one friend," the youngest girl says as they leave the room.

What she doesn't understand is that a friend, let alone many friends, is the last thing I need. To be a cat is to not need friends.

Before I'm able to drift off to sleep again, the sunbeam shifts off my bed. I decide to move to one of my other favorite spots in my house. It's in the family room, and it's a specially heated bed. The people will sit in that room and stare at it while it heats me. I appreciate the elevated position they have given me in the room, but I can't understand why they call the heated bed a "TV."

As I curl up on top, I make sure my tail doesn't hang down the front side of the TV. For some reason, the people are particular that I do not hang my tail down in front of it. I can hang it down on the other side, but not on the side they stare at. I figure it's one indulgence I can allow my subjects. Other than that, my people are loyal and obedient.

They feed me every day, even though there's plenty of food outside I enjoy catching. They've provided a private restroom indoors for me, and they clean it for me. However, I also have the great outdoors as my restroom. I have a few preferred spots in the neighbors' yards. It reminds the dogs that I'm the empress of this domain, as far as I've ventured my whole life.

The people in my house have also installed special doors that only I can fit through. They can't use them. Isn't that peculiar? I've granted this benefit so they can rest from opening my doors for me. One "cat door," as they call it, allows me to move freely from my eating room, which also contains my private bathroom and where they wash their clothes, into my garage. There's another cat door on the side of the garage which allows me out of my garage to the outdoors.

Two giant heaters rest in the garage. The amazing thing about them is that they are both mobile. The big people in my house drive them away almost every day. They must require lots of energy because the people are gone for hours at a time before bringing them back warm, and then they cool down once they're in the garage. They have a different word for them, but I don't remember it. My people spend a lot of time and effort washing and fixing these giant mobile heaters. One thing I dislike about these giant mobile heaters is that the big man person drives one of them every weekday at five o'clock sharp in the morning. I don't think he's looking out for me, and he's almost backed over me once or twice.

He's been sufficiently apologetic and frightened as I've glared at him with disapproval.

After napping on top of the TV most of the day, my favorite time arrives. The *whirrr* of the can opener floats through my house every evening, and I know the people have started preparing my food. They work so hard for my food. I rush over, not because I am desperate for the food they give me, but because I need to ensure they properly clean out the can of food into my bowl. They might miss a few morsels in the can if they don't know I'm watching their every move.

There is one thing for which I am proud of my people. They have learned to never, ever, eat my food. My food is my food alone. I don't feel sorry for them, though. I allow them to eat anything else they bring to my home. I even allow them food from my fruit trees, the grapevines in my yard, and vegetables from the garden. I only forbid them to eat food canned just for me. Other than that, they may eat of anything in my domain.

My least favorite time of day follows my favorite. At the end of the day, the people put me outside. This is the only bit of contention I have with my people. I suspect they are weak and overworked. If I were in the house at night, it would be too difficult for them to care for me adequately. I also suspect they put more of my food into cans at night. They wouldn't be able to sleep at night if I were inside because they would feel compelled to serve me. If I'm outside, they don't have to worry about me.

If only they knew what happens outside at night.

3

"The bunny is worried because one of his kids is missing," Chief reports with a yawn.

"That's all you know?" I ask the arthritic dog next door. Chief was old even when I arrived in my domain. He can hardly move, and he's always penned up, and so I always know where I can find him. Despite being a dog that is mostly blind, he typically seems to know what's going on. Even harder for me to admit, he often knows what to do. He's one of my unofficial advisers.

"Why?" Chief asks.

"You didn't notice the new kittens, or the coyote last night?"

"I am just a dog, you know?"

I know.

A snore emits from Chief's doghouse before I can continue my questioning.

I spend the rest of the night inspecting my domain, but it is quiet. Too quiet. Tonight there is no coyote, and I can't find any trace of the kittens.

The next morning, all the people leave my house in great excitement. I'm still puzzled by all that happened two nights ago with the twin kittens, Snarl, and that other weakling coyote. I'm torn between helping the kittens and letting Snarl have them. I don't want those kittens to feel as if I cared about them in any way. It would be inconvenient to interfere in the matters of coyotes. But I can't stand having anyone, especially coyotes, encroach on my territory.

The sun moves out of my favorite sunning spot. Instead of shifting to my next favorite sunning spot, I go to talk with Chief again.

After I recount to Chief what happened, he says: "That self-sacrificial attitude is definitely un-catlike." I don't know what "self-sacrificial" means, even though I know what each of the words means individually. My perplexed look tells Chief he needs to explain more. "It's something a dog would do for his master. It sounds like to me, also, that the young coyote was being tested. He had to come back with a cat, or he would be out of the pack. He's as good as dead without a pack."

"One less coyote," I observe.

"Focus on your own people's yard," Chief says. "You can't take on Snarl. Don't try to defend all the houses in the neighborhood."

"I will defend my whole domain," I say. "I'm the empress. If I don't, then who will? Could you take on Snarl?"

"No," Chief says with resignation.

I hear the grinding gears of my house's garage door opening. Without thanking Chief, I head back to my people's house.

That sound means they will return in the giant portable heater within seconds.

When I enter my house, I know something is seriously wrong. The stench of a foreign cat scorches my nostrils. Worse, it's mixed with a faint dog odor.

Before I know what's going on, the oldest girl child scoops me up in her arms and carries me to the kitchen. It all happens so fast I don't lash out in anger, but I release a low growl that indicates I am about to use my claws on her. This sort of indignity, being carried about against my will, is not typical.

When we enter the kitchen, she plops me down in the middle of the floor. Staring into my face is a sickeningly cute kitten. He is mostly orange with long fur, and he has a large white dot on his back. The white dot matches his white feet.

He looks at me.

I look at him. I narrow my eyes. I'm sure my fangs appear.

"This is Max," the children announce to me in unison. "He's your new friend."

They say this as if it's good news and I should be happy about it.

A cat doesn't need friends.

This violation of my territory without consultation shocks and offends me. My growl expands into a screech. Max's eyes widen with fear, not sure what's going to come next. He has no idea how much he should fear me. Before I have a chance to show him who is in charge of this home—even in charge of my whole territory, extending several households in all directions from this house—the oldest girl child scoops me up, opens the sliding glass door, and throws me outside.

That is no way to treat the empress of the domain.

4

When the children bring Max outside to play a few hours later, they wisely put me inside.

I cope with anger the same way I cope with any emotion I experience other than pride: I sleep. In the afternoon, I find my way to the middle child's bedroom to take a nap on his bed. I've found that he often doesn't let his two sisters in, and so I can sleep undisturbed.

But not today.

The children are still convinced I would like to meet Max and get to know him better. Somehow, they think I don't hear them. My ears twitch slightly and rotate a fraction of a millimeter to catch all that they are saying to each other.

"Okay. Hold Max close to her, but not too close so she doesn't scratch him right away."

"Will she play with Max?"

"Max will make her act younger, more like a kitten, more playful."

Upon hearing this, I shift my sleeping position so that I can direct my eyes towards them. I open my eyes a slit, but everybody else will think they're still closed.

Do these people not understand they are making a critical error? They think I want this kitten. I need nobody. I do not want to get to know this kitten.

The mattress moves under me as the children inch onto the bed. I open my eyes halfway and let out a growl just to be sure they know I'm aware of their presence. The oldest child, a girl, cradles Max in her arms.

"Princess just needs to get used to Max," she says. "Then, they'll be best friends, and they'll nap together and play together."

This is an example of why cats run the world and people don't. It would be catastrophic if people—who have no grasp of reality—were in charge.

They push Max closer. My growl hasn't warned them off. I smell an unmistakable dog odor mixed in with Max's scent. Max smells like a dog. I don't know if this is more confusing or disgusting.

Without warning, the boy child grabs Max and shoves him on top of me. Max tries to get off of me, but one of his paws presses into my belly. Nobody is allowed to touch my belly. Only a chosen person, perhaps one time per year, is permitted to touch my belly. I clench my jaw and amplify my growl, restraining myself because I don't want the people to get the idea that I'm showing any interest in Max.

If I ignore Max long enough, the people should realize I don't want him, and they will take him back to wherever he came from.

Max stumbles away from me.

The children give up on making us friends. They take Max to another room and play with him. After a few minutes, the children come back to the bed, and the oldest girl child tries to hold me down in place. The other two children try to put some people clothes on me. These clothes belong on stuffed animals and dolls!

They're trying to squeeze my limbs into a horrible plaid outfit. Max wears a matching lumberjack outfit. I bite at the oldest girl child, and she releases her grip. I must get rid of the problem.

The problem is Max.

I lunge for Max, and with a snarl like a tiger, I swipe with my claws and snap my jaws. Max responds with the thin whining meow that only kittens are capable of. A blood red slash appears on his nose. It will remind everybody who is in charge. The children scoop up Max and rush out of the room.

"We'll play doctor with him," the young girl child says.

"No, we'll play *veterinarian* with him, silly," says the middle boy child.

Apparently, playing doctor, or veterinarian, or whatever, with Max takes precedence over scolding me. I make several rotations to reposition myself and resume my nap.

I can't stop thinking about the mistakes my people are making. They treat me as if I were a lowly person. They betray me by bringing an outsider into my domain who not only is from a different domain, but who is also from a mixed area. Who would ever think of having both cats and dogs within their house?

My people disgrace me by trying to put me in their clothes. Then they try to dress me up like Max so that Max and I are somehow equal. I don't need a kitten in my house, and I definitely don't want Max. I wish I didn't have to deal with my people, just like I don't have to deal with the mess I left in my litter box a few days ago.

These thoughts race through my mind, but I still manage to fall asleep as I always do. The last thing I remember wondering is how these people are going to pack my food into a can by dinnertime.

5

I t's time to do a little research. I wonder how the people really treat Max when I'm not around. Surely they can't love him like they would a sappy puppy.

I sneak my way under the buffet in the kitchen. It's one of my favorite places to rest. There's a heating vent under the buffet, and so it gets cozy warm during the winter. It's like having a personal sunbeam without people being able to see me.

As I hide under the buffet, I watch the children play with Max. They twirl string just outside the reach of his tentatively outstretched paw. Max's eyes are wide like he's tracking a mouse, but this is just string!

The children soon switch to a small handheld device that makes a red dot dance around on the floor and on the wall. Max chases it and leaps skittishly about the room. The children's laughter only encourages him more instead of embarrassing him. I almost feel sorry for Max. The poor kitten is being treated with so much indignity.

I can't believe how well Max is tolerating the torture. He even pretends to enjoy the attention he's receiving from the people. This is far beyond what is necessary. He is simply pandering to their desires. Who would want to be treated like such an empty headed kitten?

"Has anybody seen Princess?" one asks.

"She hates Max," another answers. "You won't find her around here."

"I think she is too afraid to admit she might actually end up liking Max."

"She'll come running soon," says the big man person as he walks in. "Just wait and see."

Don't people understand that cats are mysterious and indiscernible? People are foolish to think that they could understand a cat. I don't know why I even try to set them straight.

My tummy growls.

Right then, as if by magic, I hear the can opener *whirrr* and I rush out from under the buffet and straight to the nearby counter. The big man person opens my can of food.

I grant one expectant meow, my only meow for the day, to encourage him. However, if he could read my mind, he would know I am gloating at how well I have him trained.

Just as my tummy growled, he started to fetch my food.

I wonder how my people can be so hard of hearing and yet manage to get my food every evening exactly when they hear my tummy growl.

6

Max stretches out his paw towards a flower's leaf twitching in the breeze. He's on his back, apparently too lazy and careless to even pursue a plant.

I glower at Max from on top of my fence. I have had to teach this intruder difficult lessons. I have taught Max where he is allowed to sleep (not on my bed), when he is permitted to eat (after me), and where he may go to the bathroom.

Max interrupts my fuming indignation against my people for bringing him into my house without permission. Max crouches in the grass. Something has his attention. My eyes search several feet in front of Max, but I can't quite make out what it is. I hear a light *tink tink*. Something moves in the grass. It must be those infernal twins. I don't see them. I only hear their collars.

Max springs from his crouch and pounces. He misses, but he pounces again seconds later. He misses again. The twins must have tied their collars to a string, and now they are pulling on the string, sending Max on a chase. The string wraps around trees and the swing set. I don't know where the string ends. One of the twins must be watching from nearby, and one of them must be pulling as Max chases it.

I hear the tinkling as they pull the string a few feet, and then Max jumps. Before he lands, they pull it again, and Max has to go chasing after it again.

Max is content to chase the collars around my backyard for some time. But then the collars disappear through a partial tunnel that goes under a chain-link fence. Max is small enough to fit under the chain-link fence (I think I could fit through if I had to), and then he's on the chase again.

I move closer to follow the action.

After Max comes up on the other side of the chain-link fence, he trips on something. Max goes rolling in a ball of orange and white fur. Dust puffs up around him.

Muffled laughter escapes from one of the twins. It sounds like Tweedledee. Max gets up dazed and looks around. He licks himself, pretending nothing has happened. Max walks to my back yard.

Now I'm angry at Tweedledee and Tweedledum. How dare they mock Max, part of my kingdom and my household? Max may be a fool, but he is my fool. I'm going to teach those twins a lesson once I find them at the end of the string.

I spot Tweedledee rushing back to her house. She was the twin hiding, monitoring Max's chase and somehow signaling Tweedledum from afar to pull on the string. I will find both of them at the end of the string.

I jump down from my post, and I rush under the chain-link fence. After I emerge on the other side, I'm careful to leap with grace over the tripwire that caught Max as I approach the tinkling collars. The twins stop laughing, and the collars start moving again.

No matter. I will chase these collars, and I will find the twins at the end of the string.

Max must have been near the end of the course set by the twins. The collars go around one tree and then race directly towards the sliding glass door on the back of the twins' people's house.

I accelerate towards the house.

I'm going to leap into the twins' house, and I'm going to scratch them so hard they will wish they only had eight lives.

The collars at the end of the string are only a split second away from entering the twins' house. I leap to overtake them and fly into the twins' house.

Thwack!

My head strikes some sort of unseen forcefield protecting the twins' house, and I crash to the ground. I look up, stunned, and laying on my back. The twins' owner comes into view inside the house on the opposite side of the force field. She holds a cloth in one hand and a clear plastic bottle full of blue liquid in the other.

She must see me.

"Who left this door open a crack?" she says. "Poor thing. I guess I cleaned the sliding glass door well enough."

My head hurts, and I think I hear the twins' laughter coming from their house. Maybe it's the throbbing in my head. Either way, I vow to get revenge on those twins as I stagger back to my house.

7

I spend most of my days alternating between sleeping and almost sleeping. I ponder how to conquer Snarl, how to catch more birds and mice, how to teach Max a lesson, and how to prevent other intruders from entering my domain.

Today, however, I dream. I dream about Patches. I had a crush on Patches. He had many admirable qualities. He was quite a bit older than me, and I was constantly trying to get his attention. He was too busy ruling his domain to pay attention to me. He was a visionary leader.

I dream about Patches because my heart broke the day Patches went missing. He simply disappeared. He went out one night, and then he was missing the next morning. It ruined me. I could hardly function. I hate to admit it, but I even peed on the rug in the people's house after Patches disappeared.

It was so bad, the people took me to the veterinarian. Apparently, the vet knows how to mend broken hearts.

So why am I dreaming of Patches now? I dream we are eating fish together. But then, I'm cruelly awoken.

It's Max, of course.

Doesn't he know that cats sleep during the day?

I admit, I'm more angry that Patches is gone than I am at Max for waking me. I lash out with my claws. Max has a scratch on his nose, and now I've taken a patch of his fur. Max leaps off my bed.

Max's fur is an ugly mix of orange and white, and it's long. That means that he sheds all over my house. Perhaps the worst thing about the shedding is that my people have to spend extra time cleaning up Max's fur instead of caring for me.

I sense Max's presence in the room even though he's not on the bed. He's nearby. I get the feeling that he still thinks he can win me over. Well, he can keep on dreaming. As a matter of fact, speaking of dreams, I think I have an idea. I wonder if I could use that new coyote as an ally against Snarl.

Hmmmm.

Something to think about.

Max might also be a useful ally for me. If only I could train Max to carry out my plans. I'm just not sure if he's worth the hassle. The hardest part would be convincing Max I actually like him and want him to get better.

I feel a slight pressure somewhere on my bed. Max has leapt back up onto the bed. I feel his kitten-soft steps on the bed.

Max lurks too close. I let out a deep growl. I can see through my barely opened eyes that Max is confused. He must be wondering how I knew he was too close since I have given no indication of being awake other than my rumblingly low growl.

Max takes a few steps back.

I stop growling.

Max inches closer.

A pause, and he moves slowly again.

I restart my growl.

Max scoots back.

We continue like this for a few minutes. Eventually, I steer Max with my growls to the one spot on my bed he is allowed to sleep. The people laid a towel on the foot of my bed so that Max's fur doesn't sully it. I sense Max lay down on the towel. I open my eyes, and they lock with his. I don't have to say anything, because my eyes say it all: "You may only sleep there."

Am I getting soft in my old age?

I can't believe I'm allowing Max to sleep on my bed, even if it is at the very foot of the bed and far away for me. I let the big people sleep in it at night while I'm outside so that they can warm it up, but even the children people are not allowed to sleep in my bed.

I use all of my energy to prevent myself from pouncing on Max. I may need him to go along with my plan to get rid of Snarl. He could be useful, at least as bait.

Max is wide-eyed in the crouching position, and it pulls me out of my internal dreaming and plotting. His eyes dart back and forth as if he's watching a game of Ping-Pong. His eyes follow my twitching tail. I guess it does twitch when I ruminate.

The youngest girl person walks into the room and sees Max's pouncing position and yells, "Max! No!"

But it's too late. Max pounces at my tail while I'm still plotting to defeat Snarl, and so my reaction time is slow. Max gets in a few good bites and scratches, but they only serve to infuriate me. A sharp *yowl* and a few slashes with my claws, and Max's belly is scratched as the girl child pulls Max off the bed.

She scolds Max as she carries him out of the room.

"You should know better than to play with Princess, especially when she's sleeping."

About time those people finally correct Max! I've known it since they brought him here: he needs scolding and discipline. I was afraid those people would commit treason and blame me for what just happened.

The youngest girl child sticks her head back into the room.

"Why are you such a meanie?" Her eyes are red and puffy from crying. "You are going to die with no friends." She slams the door, but yells from outside, "I hope a coyote eats you!"

Hopefully that incident will teach Max I'm in charge. The worst part is that I allowed Max, even if only for a few minutes, to sleep on my bed.

If I'm going to make Max think I like him, even a little bit, I'll show him where the best hiding places and sleeping places are. There are only a few ideal spots that are comfy, warm, and private. I'll teach him my less ideal spots. I will also teach him how to hunt for birds and mice. Such things come naturally for a specimen like me, but Max is not nearly the cat I am. He couldn't catch a mouse if it scurried into his mouth.

8

Because I'm making a universe altering decision, I should talk it over with my one trusted adviser: Chief.

I understand he's a dog, but he has accepted my position as empress from day one. Unsure of how he's acquired any wisdom as a dog, I figure he's lived long enough and filtered out all of the goofy things he thinks as a dog. What remains is wisdom. Even a dog stumbles upon a bit of insight every now and then. After his long life, he's gathered a few insights along the way.

"I'm thinking of taking on an apprentice," I say.

"Who could be so worthy of that?" Chief asks, hardly moving from halfway outside his doghouse. I sit on the fence, looking down at him. He usually doesn't make it more than halfway out his doghouse each day. (I would like to point out that my house has multiple rooms and facilities for the people —like special bathrooms just for them—whereas the dog in my domain has a tiny one-bedroom house without amenities for people, cats, or dogs.)

"It's not a matter of worthiness," I say. "It's a matter of practicality."

Chief raises an eyebrow at that.

"I don't need *help*," I clarify. "An apprentice would be more convenient, and it would allow me to focus more of my time on important matters."

"I'm honored you would consider me, but I must respectfully decline."

I suspect a hint of sarcasm.

"Heavens no!" I say. "Not you." Chief withdraws from my reaction slightly, and I know I have to make up ground in my relationship with Chief. "You are a fount of wisdom, and I will need you to advise my apprentice. If you were my apprentice, who would advise you? If my apprentice doesn't listen to me, then when he asks you and you agree with me, he will learn quickly to trust me."

"Let me guess. One of those new kittens will be your apprentice. How 'bout the boy kitten from the house behind yours? He was heroic offering himself in the place of his sister. His name is Tweedledum."

"Fitting name, but he would be my second choice."

"Who is your first choice? His sister, Tweedledee?"

"Max," I say.

"With everything I've seen and heard, it seems like you view him as nothing but an insulting intrusion into your kingdom."

"He is exactly that," I say. "He's flawed, but he will be useful to me." Chief raises his eyebrow again. I wonder if he's trying to say something when he does that.

"My question is this: How can I convince Max that I like him when I so obviously detest him? I'm going to need him to obey me if I'm going to use him as..." I almost say, "bait," but I catch myself. "If I'm going to use him, that's all."

Chief's eyebrow is still raised.

"Trust is hard to earn," Chief says after he lowers his eyebrows.

"I just want the goober to think that I like him, just a little bit. I don't care if he trusts me. Regardless of what he thinks, I'm in charge," I clarify.

"Think about somebody you don't trust. Do you care if somebody you don't trust likes you?" Chief asks. "It only works if there's trust."

"I'm the empress of this domain. What choice does Max—anybody—have other than to trust me?"

Chief's eyebrows don't shift a whisker as he stares at me. I must not be on the right track.

"Why do you really want an apprentice, anyhow?" Chief asks. "And don't tell me—"

"To get rid of Snarl."

"Snarl? You remember Patches, don't you?" Chief asks. Chief must have seen my jaw hit the fence. "I think it's about time you learned the truth about Patches."

"Patches ... disappeared," I say. My throat strained to get the last word out.

Does Chief somehow know I was dreaming about Patches?

"Nope," Chief says. "Patches went to fight Snarl, and Patches lost."

"Snarl killed Patches?"

Chief gives a slow nod in affirmation.

This is the encouragement I need. At first, I only wanted to protect my domain from Snarl, but now, I want revenge.

Max is going to help me get it.

9

"I don't think Princess would have done anything like that," I hear the big woman person say on the phone a few days later. I listen a little more, and I sense that the person on the other end of the conversation isn't proud of me or happy about me.

This confuses me. Why else would somebody call my house and talk about me other than to offer me praise? (I did do an excellent job of catching a bird earlier today. I offered it to my people as a gift, but they were too humble to accept it from me.)

I'm also surprised that it's the big woman person who's talking on the phone. I thought that was the job of the oldest girl child. As far as I can tell, she spends hours on the telephone talking with people, and her parents are constantly telling her to, "Get off the phone."

The TV warms my tummy, but the conversation in the kitchen has my interest. I rotate one ear slightly to focus in on it. The big woman person hangs up the telephone on the wall.

"The neighbors said Princess got into their garbage cans outside and made a huge mess," the big woman person says to the big man person.

"Princess wouldn't do that," the big man person says.

Exactly right! I own this place. Why would I go play in the trash?

"They found a big tuft of gray cat fur at the scene of the crime," the big woman person says. "Princess is the only gray cat—tabby or otherwise—around."

"That's not like Princess," the big man person says.

"I apologized and said that if Princess does it again, we would lock her in the laundry room or garage at night," the big woman person says.

"Princess would not be happy about that."

That is an understatement bigger than the mess I did leave on their back step. I would not tolerate detainment.

I know I didn't play in their trash. Another gray tabby has infiltrated my domain without my knowledge. There have been no new pets since the twin kittens. This happened right under my nose, and it irritates me like a new application of flea powder. I must step up my nightly surveillance.

I go to consult with Chief again.

"There haven't been any new pets since the twin kittens, right?" I ask Chief from atop the fence, looking down into his pen.

"You're right about that," he confirms.

"Especially not any gray tabbies?"

"Nope."

"Have you noticed any strange cats in my domain the last few nights?"

"Nope."

This perplexes me. If there's another gray tabby this stealthy, is it possible I have a long lost identical twin? If so, what would happen if we fought each other?

I need to be extra vigilant tonight.

"I did notice somebody else, though," Chief says.

"What?" I ask. "Who?"

"I'm surprised you don't already know. Buck paid me a visit last night at dusk."

"Who is Buck?"

"He's the young coyote Snarl tested by forcing him to take one of the twin kittens," Chief says.

"You didn't attack him or report him to me immediately?" I ask, getting my fur in a dander.

"You were busy eating your canned food at the time, and I figured you didn't want to be interrupted," Chief says. He makes a good point. Chief is the only one in my domain who doesn't cower when I challenge him. "Besides," Chief continues, "I think you might be able to use Buck for your purposes. Sort of like a spy."

"To be a spy," I say, "one must be cunning, sly, full of deception, patient, and yet able to take decisive action at key moments. Essentially, you have to be a cat. This coyote, however, is worse than a dog. No offense."

"None taken. Ever," says Chief.

"Also, I was aware of Buck's visit," I say, admittedly bending the truth beyond recognition. "I was testing you to see if you would tell me."

Chief blinks, apparently not persuaded.

"Why do you call him 'Buck,' anyways?" I ask. "How'd you learn his name?"

"I gave him the name," Chief says. "Unless you're a leader

like Snarl, coyotes usually go by '*Alpha*,' '*Beta*,' and so on in their pack, but Buck was actually '*Psi*.' Not worthy enough to have the honor of being '*Omega*,'" Buck explains. "I figured he was a young buck, so I started calling him 'Buck.'"

"You realize that giving something a personal name implies you are giving it inherent value, don't you?" I point out.

"To be useful to us, he needs to think he has some value," Chief says.

"Tell me about Buck," I demand.

"He came to me at dusk, seeking my help. Since I'm a dog, he hoped I would have mercy on him. We are supposedly distant cousins, but I don't think even my inbred second cousins from across the tracks really have a family tree that contains coyotes—"

"Get to the point," I cut in. "And please, if you ever name another coyote, please name it, 'Roadkill.'"

"Hey, that's a good one," Chief says. "Buck thinks Snarl is going to kick him out of the pack. A coyote without a pack is a dead coyote," says Chief.

"Perfect. That's the best kind of coyote. This is why coyotes never gain power. They fight amongst themselves so much."

"Buck wanted advice on how he could get some people to take him in as a pet."

The audacity of this concept makes me feel like I just saw a flying fish. There's nothing a coyote could offer to people, and so why would the people want a pet coyote? People offer me several useful services, and I keep them around so that they feel like they are contributing to a greater good, but it doesn't work the other way around. How ignorant of that coyote. Chief senses I think this is idiotic, probably from my rolling eyes.

"I've also noticed something," Chief goes on. "I'm sure you

noticed as well. Those new twin kittens are exceedingly mischievous."

"What makes you say that? Let's see if you report to me accurately," I say, even though I only know a part of their mischief.

"I saw those two twin kittens mess with a birdfeeder so that the chipmunks and squirrels could get into it to eat all the bird feed. Then, when the people in the house would look at the birdfeeder in hopes of seeing a bird, the twins would snicker with laughter. They didn't want to use the birdfeeder to catch birds, squirrels, or chipmunks. They wanted to ruin the bird-watching."

Suddenly, Chief and I both hear some rustling in the bushes nearby. I instinctively leap up into a nearby tree to hide.

Who could it be?

The twins, Tweedledee and Tweedledum, come out of the bushes rolling and wrestling with each other. They stop wrestling long enough to saunter past Chief's pen. While passing, they say, "Hey, Chief. How's it going? Anything new, old man?"

"My paw sure is hurting. It's gonna' rain soon," says Chief.

The twins continue on, and they're heading in the direction of my house. Every bone in my body tells me to leap down on top of them and scratch them with my claws, but I'm curious as to where Tweedledee and Tweedledum might be going, and exactly what they might be planning to do.

I follow Tweedledee and Tweedledum into my own yard. From up above in the trees, I see what they're looking at. They see Max inside my house walking on the piano. He is such a klutz. The children inside laugh hysterically at Max. It is a disgrace to cats everywhere, yet the people seem to love it, and Max thrives on it.

"Let's find more of Princess' fur," says Tweedledee.

"I'm sure we'll find some somewhere," says Tweedledum.

"Chief said it was going to rain soon."

"The rain would wash away the evidence."

A few seconds later, I watch Tweedledee and Tweedledum leave my yard. Now I know for sure that there isn't a sinister gray tabby invading my domain, and I don't have a long-lost identical twin. It's Tweedledee and Tweedledum who are plotting against me.

I go inside my house for the evening, eat my canned food as usual, but this night the people decide to keep me inside, locked in the garage. At first, I'm angry because I know nobody has messed with the neighbors' garbage, but the people say it's so that I don't get in a fight with Max.

Max will spend his first night outside. The people figure Max is big enough to face most dangers on his own, but he's not big enough to defend himself against me in case we get in a fight.

This leaves me powerless to stop anything Tweedledee and Tweedledum may attempt tonight. There's no hope Max will stop them. I'm betting Max will try to make friends with Buck and get eaten instead. That wouldn't be the worst, but I need Max for my plan. At least for now.

The next morning my jaw drops far enough for a mouse to crawl in. I'm shocked.

Max is still alive.

The people aren't surprised, but they are both thrilled and relieved, cheering him on as he struts into the house. I run out of the house as soon as I can; I need to talk to Chief to find out what Max and the twins were up to.

"What did Max do last night?" I casually ask after I hop up onto the fence surrounding Chief's pen. I want to know what Max did, but I don't want it to seem like I care about Max. My eyes follow the robins in the nearby tree so Chief thinks I'm uninterested.

"Nothing," Chief says. Something tells me he's holding out.

I decide I have all day to find out what Max really did at night. If Chief won't tell me, Max will.

When I get back home, the people are discussing whether

or not they should put me and Max outside at the same time at night.

"She's going to beat up and torture Max," protests the youngest girl child.

She's probably right about that.

"He can't survive on his own, though," counters the boy child.

He's right about that, for sure. Max was lucky last night. Max will try to make friends with Buck, or worse, Snarl, if I'm not with him at night.

The people go back and forth about it until the big man person finally makes a decision that is horrible: Max will go outside by himself for a week. He will then be accustomed to the yard at night without interference from me, and if there's danger, he can hide in our fenced yard.

The nights creep by; Max goes out while I stay in. I ask Max vaguely each morning how the nights have gone and what he has done. He never tells me. He only says that he likes lying under the lilac bush.

Chief also won't tell me what Max does at night. I know he knows, but he won't tell me. I'm tempted to demand that he tell me, but I prefer my subjects to serve me out of gratitude and willingness. I will give Chief some time so he doesn't feel coerced to serve me.

Finally, after a week, I am able to walk my domain at night. I'm sure I have lots of work to catch up on. First, I'll ask Chief one last time what Max did at night all last week. At least I can't be blamed for any of Tweedledee's and Tweedledum's mischief since I was caged like an animal at night.

I have a few guesses about what Max did. Perhaps he spent

the time trying to win over the pizza delivery boys with his pathetic meow. It persuades people because they find it cute, but Max didn't find it nearly as persuasive with birds. Maybe he spent a lot of time walking on the top of a fence. That wouldn't normally be a challenge for a cat, but Max is not your average cat. He's far below average. He needs practice to walk on a fence.

Chief's response, however, confuses me.

"You already know what Max did all week," Chief says.

"Did he try to make friends with mice?"

"Nope."

"Did he try to drive one of those portable heaters?"

Chief gives me a confused look.

"At least he didn't chase one of them like a dog would," I say. "Did he chase his own tail like a dog? No offense."

"Nope. No offense taken."

"Then, what did Max do?"

Chief still doesn't answer.

I hate it when he gets quiet and cryptic. He's no Yoda, that's for sure.

"He didn't—" I start in fear "—he didn't play with Tweedledee and Tweedledum, did he?"

"Nope. He was just collecting things."

"Collecting things? Like what?" I ask.

"Amongst other things, he was collecting his own fur."

"That is... abnormal," I say, and I've heard a lot of weird things since we've gotten Max.

Max has asked me things like: Why does my shadow follow me everywhere? How come nobody is friends with the skunk? Why do you let your people live in your house at all? Is it okay to eat grass?

"Because summer's almost over, he knows he's gonna' stop shedding," says Chief.

"And he needs to save his fur for later?" I ask. It's impossible to outthink a scatterbrain like Max because he's so unpredictable.

"So loony he's baffling," I conclude.

"There are other positive attributes besides intelligence," Chief says.

Like humility before those in authority over you, I think to myself.

It's time I visit this lilac bush Max spent so much time under during the last week.

Max is right. It is a nice spot, I recall. I guess I can let him have it for now. What I need to do is observe Max for a while. Study him and see what he does. He has permission to use this lilac bush for now. In the future, I'll give him jobs and responsibilities to help maintain my rule over my domain (not that I would really give him anything too important because he'll probably mess it up). For now, I want to see what he will do if I don't tell him what to do.

When I arrive at the lilac bush, Max is relaxing under its branches. So far, that fits with what I've heard, even if it's completely abnormal for a cat. I want to go prowling, but I need to watch Max. As if sleeping all day isn't enough. Now he needs to sleep under the lilac bush at night? Although, he does spend an awful lot of time playing with the children during the day. Max looks at some bugs with interest. His tail twitches as he watches them. He licks his chops, and then he looks away as if he's forgotten about the bugs.

And now Max ... oh gross ... is using my lilac bush as a toilet.

Add that to my list of duties as empress: train Max where to go to the bathroom. Has he been peeing in my yard all week?

My yard is not your toilet, I say to myself.

The sun is about to come up, and all I've seen Max do is go to the bathroom under my lilac bush, look at some bugs, sleep, and... that's it. At least he didn't collect his own shed fur, as weird as that is.

Suddenly, a large crash erupts from the twins' yard. I have to go see what happened, despite how fascinating it has been to study Max in my domain at night.

11

I rush over to the neighbors' house. I arrive in time to see the twins, Tweedledee and Tweedledum, sneak through their cat door into their house. I immediately know what is going on. I must not let anybody see me here, or they will blame me for the mess.

I sprint towards my own house.

As I dash home, Max comes running directly at me. Before I even have time to ask him what in the world he thinks he's doing, he rushes past me, without hardly even noticing me.

Fool rushing into trouble, I think. *But I'm not going to stop him.*

I make it back to my own garage and enter the house. I need my people to notice me. Then they will know I am not the one who knocked over the neighbors' trashcans. The big man person is up quite early this morning. I strut around the kitchen with my head and tail held high to make sure he notices me.

I'm relieved when the youngest girl child walks in, sleepy eyed and whiny, and says, "Oh, hi, Princess." I walk right up to her and rub against her leg. There's no way she's going to forget me.

Who could accuse a regal cat such as me of playing in other people's trash?

"Where's Max?" the child asks with an edge of anxiety.

"I'm sure he'll be in soon," answers the big man person.

"You don't think... A coyote got him, do you? And he was so young," says the girl child.

All this talk about Max is rubbing me the wrong way. He's not even deserving to be a cat, and he's probably silly enough to be playing in the neighbors' trash at this moment. I hear the big man person crunching on his food for breakfast as he sits at the table. I walk over to him to rub myself against his leg to remind him that I'm here and not playing in the neighbors' trash.

I'm proud of these people. Even after offering their food to me, they still have enough resources to eat food themselves, even if it is just dry food that they add milk to. I don't remember the last time I had milk. I must've been a kitten.

Just then, a thumping noise echoes from the front of the house. Max has banged into the garage door that was only partially shut, and then he comes trundling into the kitchen galloping like a three-legged dog.

The girl child squeals. "Max! You're back!"

She runs over to Max. I'm staring at Max wide-eyed, and the big man person stops crunching his food. However, just as the girl child bends over to scoop Max up, he unleashes a wretch that sounds like it came from a three-legged St. Bernard. A gray hairy wad of vomit launches out of his throat faster than he came into the kitchen. It splats right on to the kitchen floor.

Before we can all react in disgust, the phone rings, even this early in the morning. I hide under the buffet, shocked by all that I just saw. Now I have to teach Max not to puke in my house in addition to not peeing in my yard. There are plenty of other good places to go puke if you absolutely have to, but why does Max have to do it in my house like a dog—even a three-legged dog, at that?

The big man person answers the phone and winces at the gray pile of cat puke on the floor. What I hear tells me what I already know: the neighbors' trash cans have been knocked over and strewn about again. I prepare to walk around the kitchen to remind the people again that I would never sink to such lows. I feel my anger well up at those two twins, Tweedledee and Tweedledum, who dare to try to get me in trouble with the people.

Instead, the big person says into the phone, "I'm really sorry. Max is sick. He just threw up all over the kitchen, and so maybe he wasn't feeling well, and maybe he wasn't thinking straight when he got into your trash."

The big man person is still talking on the phone, and he's listening, and then I see concern spread over his face as his eyes widen slightly.

"You think Max might have eaten *that* in your trash, and that's why he's sick? Oh dear."

I can't stand the big man person's concern for Max. Max simply had a common fur ball, and that was all. However, I am getting excited now that I realize my people may take Max to the vet. A vet is that person who always tells me what I already know: I am a perfect cat. Do they need a vet to tell them that Max is lacking a brain?

Later that morning, after all of the people are awake and eating food (and they've cleaned my kitchen floor), I head outside to pace the fence angrily. I'm going to make sure those twins learn their place in my domain. They would be in my doghouse if I had one. I just have to let that coyote Buck get them when I have the chance.

I watch as the people drive away from the house in one of the large portable heaters. They're probably taking Max to the vet. Those vet visits, especially emergency ones, are expensive. I'm not sure what "expensive" means, but the people talk like it's a big deal. However, they've always done even the tough things for me, like handle expensive vet visits.

For Max, I'm not so sure.

A few minutes later, I go outside to tell Chief what happened. I recount the commotion and cat puke. Chief says, "So how do you think Max was able to puke up a gray fur ball? And why was he running to the trash cans instead of away from them?"

Chief can be confusing at times, and I think maybe in his old age, he's getting confused himself.

"Do you think, maybe," Chief continues, "that the twins put your fur by the trash cans before they knocked them over so that it would look like you knocked them over?"

"But then Max himself licked up my fur..." I say.

Baffling.

"Max saved you," Chief says with too much satisfaction in his voice.

12

It's time to teach Max how to be my subordinate in ruling my domain. If he's going to help me defeat Snarl, he has to know the basics. The easiest way to start training him is to teach him how to catch birds. Every cat should know how to do that, even without training.

How hard can it be?

I will expect him to give back to me at least ten percent of what he catches in my territory. I think that's rather generous. But first, I want to see what sort of techniques and strategies Max uses in order to catch birds. I fear he's going to be horrible at it.

I discover I am wrong. He is beyond horrible. He catches birds like a two-legged St. Bernard dog.

I might as well enjoy a good sunbeam as I observe Max, so I hide myself in one of my favorite sunning spots inside. I lay down just inside a sliding glass door that looks out into my backyard. I watch Max through the slits of my eyes, pretending to be asleep. What I see is appalling. Max sits on his haunches at the bottom of the willow tree, and he looks up at the birds, mostly robins, who are fluttering about the branches.

"Meow?" he begs pitifully. And then a few seconds later, "Meeeooooow?" again, but a bit more drawn out and full of desperation. He is asking the birds to do something. Worse, he is begging the birds to come to him. I didn't expect Max to be this horrible at catching birds. How is he ever going to be an ally against Snarl?

I restrain myself from going outside to correct him and to teach those robins a lesson. Max will be willing to listen and to learn after the robins thoroughly humiliate him. I watch his humiliation increase. A few of the robins nosedive and then squawk at him before the next dive. Mockery drips from their chirps.

The indignity is becoming too much. I must rescue the honor of cats everywhere. Otherwise, birds will come from all over the world to make a mockery of me and of my domain instead of trembling at the honor of being my prey and sport.

I get up without anybody noticing and exit my house through the garage so that I can sneak up onto the fence. Once I'm on the fence, I make my way over to the willow tree. I imagine myself catching all of those robins off guard as they focus on Max. I will turn them into a puff of feathers and blood. They won't know what hit them.

Such a display of feline power will awe Max and convince him he needs to take his cat-ness seriously instead of acting like a pathetic dog. Max cowers from the birds. He lies down, even exposing his stomach as he rolls onto his back and meows to plead for mercy. He begs the robins to leave him alone. It's as if he's being bullied by these robins. Max makes no advances, no attacks, and he's not making a tactical retreat. A few brave robins peck out tufts of his fur.

Max would probably give himself to Snarl if he asked. What is going on inside his furry pea-sized brain that makes him ask the birds to come down so he can catch them?

The birds grow in boldness after each round of nosedives and taunts. The leader of a large robin family, a proud male, does not trust Max. He refuses to swoop too close at first, but his trajectory inches closer with each dive.

I know this male robin. He's lived in my domain for generations, and he is a worthy robin. His family has provided me much food and sport. He knows his place in the pecking order, and I would rather not have to catch him. I don't want to lose a great robin family in my domain.

He lines up to lead one last dive-bombing charge at Max. His orange chest puffs out. I weigh the loss of a noble robin family in my domain against showing off my superiority to the spectators. This is the perfect time to capture the father robin. He chirps to the other male robins, at least nine in all, to join him for a dive-bombing run at Max.

I inch along to a lower branch on the tree. The robins swoop down in an attack formation. The world slows down around me as I focus; I time my jump. I launch into the air to intercept the lead robin. Air rushes by me as I knife through the sky towards my prey with hungry jaws and expectant claws. I will catch the robin in midair just before he strikes Max with his talons.

"It's a trap!" the father robin yells to warn his fellow dive-bombers off. All the robins pull up at the last second and alter course.

Max must have tipped them off! I think in midair.

A white glue-like substance that encases their brown seedy poop hurls through the air at Max, but it strikes me instead as I arrive at the location of their original target.

Those robins projectile-pooped on me!

The robins settle in the upper branches, and I land, coated in their poop, standing before Max.

"You see what humiliation I save you from?" I hiss at Max, not knowing if I'm more angry at the birds or at Max.

"Thank you! Thank you! Thank you!" Max says. "Foolish me thought I had finally lured the large robin in close enough to capture him, but now I see that they were just going to poop on me. Thank you!"

I stare at Max. Max stares at me. I can't believe it.

"You speak?" I say, partly a question and partly an expression of astonishment.

I forget the humiliation of wearing bird poop destined for Max because a loud metallic crash in the front yard breaks my stunned silence. I rush over to the fence and leap on top of it just in time to see a small coyote running away. It looks over its shoulder at me as if he is getting away with something. It must be Buck.

It's not even dusk yet, but the coyotes are active. Something is amiss in my domain.

13

Now that I've spotted Buck the coyote in my domain, I need to train Max faster. He needs to know more than just the basics of bird catching. He needs to know how to protect my domain. He must defend it like a real cat, even though he can't catch birds like a real cat. Max could at least raise the alarm if an intruder comes instead of asking for a belly rub.

I come up to Max the next day, and I say, "You will learn how to defend my domain. You may die doing so, but such is your purpose in life." You have to make things crystal-clear for those who are not very intelligent.

"Does laying in the sun protect your domain?" asks Max.

"No, and I care not if any people invade. I have my own people to handle them, but I am concerned about other cats, dogs, and worst of all, coyotes."

"What's a coyote?" asks Max. "Sounds like something you put on the grill."

"Coyotes are worse than dogs," I answer. "They are uncouth dogs who exist solely to humiliate cats. The enmity and selfishness of coyotes is astonishing. At least dogs like Chief understand their role in nature. Coyotes are the cancer of nature. Come with me so I can teach you the basic tactics of coyote defense."

Max follows me into the twins' yard. From atop a fence, we watch the twins play with an ant pile. They inspect the ants going this way and that, sniffing them, and occasionally pawing at them.

"Oooh," Max says, "that looks fun." My glare tells him he can't join them. We hop down to hide under a bush. The twins haven't noticed us.

"The most common tactic for cats," I start to explain to Max, "is to arch your back, puff up your tail, stick out your claws, and let out horrible hisses and screeches. Be sure to start with a low and rumbling growl to scare others away. It's a warning, like the rattle of a rattlesnake."

"How does that help against coyotes?"

"It makes you look bigger and scarier than you really are. It's something you need a lot of help with."

"There's no way a coyote would fall for that," Max says, but then he looks at me. I've transformed. I've metamorphosed into a beast the size of a small bear. My eyes glow yellow, my fangs and claws unsheathe, and with one sharp hiss, I send Max running back home. I follow him to my house. The youngest girl child coddles him in her arms. Max shakes, his eyes as large as my food dishes.

The girl child puts Max down, and he meows to be let inside. I chuckle to myself.

Later that night I think Max must be trying to hide so that

the people won't throw him outside for the night. He doesn't realize I am what scared him. My people finally find Max drinking water out of the toilet just like a dog (I shudder), and they throw Max out for the night. He stays by the sliding glass door at the back of the house, still terrified of the bear beast that sent him running earlier.

"Maybe a coyote scared him," I hear one of the people say while Max peers inside through the sliding glass door, repeatedly meowing to be let back in.

I slink closer to Max, but I don't come out of the shadows yet. From the shadows I ask, "Were you frightened by a coyote, Max?"

I already know the answer.

"No. I was afraid this bear-like monster had eaten you up, and I ran for my life!"

"How do you think such a beast could enter my domain without permission?" I ask.

"*You* let him into your domain?"

I walk into the light so that Max can see me, and I'm puffed up as before, but I'm not hissing, and I'm not showing all of my claws and fangs. Max intensifies his meows. I shrink to my normal self and retract my claws.

"It's magic!" Max gasps. "Are you a were-bear?"

"What's a were-bear?" I ask, knowing I don't really want to hear his goofy explanation.

"You know, a cat who turns into a bear every full moon."

"Where do you come up with these ideas? Never mind. Don't tell me. Now you show me what you've got. All you do is arch your back, puff your tail, show your fangs and claws, and *hiss*."

Max arches his back as much as he can, and he makes some

of his already long and gloppy fur stick out a little more, but he can't give a good hiss and bare his fangs. Instead, it looks to me he's showing his teeth to the vet for a checkup. Max emits a purr, not the growl I am hoping for.

"You look like one of those kids in a family photo who's being made to smile or you won't get any ice cream," I say. "We need to come up with something else for you. Or you won't have a chance, even against a coyote like Buck."

14

One night later, it's time to show Max how cats can defeat any opponent in a fight. With this technique, we can conquer large and terrifying animals, even a coyote. We can shame them so that they never come back, and we can hurt them so much that they will die a slow and painful death. I relish the day when I will do that to Patches' killer, Snarl. He's too wily to ever let me attack him in that way, however. He knows too much, and he would never allow himself to be vulnerable like that. Honestly, in my nightmares, I'm afraid that he's the one opponent who won't succumb to this attack.

I explain to Max how a cat leaps onto an opponent's back and bites into the scruff of the back of the neck and holds on with the protruding front paws while scratching furiously with the rear paws. "No matter what, never let go until the coyote is defeated," I say.

"You're not going to demonstrate on me, are you?" Max asks.

"I don't want your fur in my mouth," I say. "Let's have you practice on Chief. At least get in the right position so that you know what it's supposed to be like." I lead Max over to Chief, and he agrees because Max is his buddy by now.

Max clumsily mounts Chief's back. Max isn't very good at jumping or moving in general because he must have three left paws and only one right paw. Max delicately bites the back of Chief's neck, but Max finds Chief to be so large, warm, and cozy that I'm afraid Max is going to settle in to take a nap. Chief lets out a few moans as if he's getting a back massage from Max.

"What do you call this attack maneuver, anyways?" Chief calls out to me in between moans as he enjoys his complimentary massage.

In my disgust, I have a flash of brilliance.

"When executed properly, I call it, The Guillotine."

Max's poor practice run confirms that I will have to destroy Snarl on my own, and Max will most likely be lost. But I am certain of one thing: Snarl's head will roll.

15

I will tell Max a secret, one I've never told anybody. I have never told Chief about it, and I never told Patches about it. My people don't know that I know about it. Then Max will trust me and willingly play his role in my plan to defeat Snarl.

Here's the secret: my people installed a button that makes the garage door open and shut, as if by magic, whenever the button is pressed. Even if my people decide to lock the cat door on the side of my garage, I could still circumvent it. The power of the button is admittedly symbolic in large part; animals often do not wield the power of machines.

As empress, I do have power over machines with this button.

"How did you find out about it?" Max asks me.

"Nothing is hidden from me in my domain," I say. "One morning, I was sleeping on top of the large portable heater in the garage, and the big man person came out to open the garage and to start the portable heater to get it ready for him to go to work. He pressed this button, and immediately the garage door began to open. He doesn't know that I know about it."

"Why do you want to keep your knowledge a secret?"

"Do you realize how important this is?" I say. "What would happen if Snarl got one of those buttons? He could enter my house unhindered. Besides, these buttons should only be used if there is an emergency. Otherwise, the people would know that we know, and they would hide the buttons. The people have other buttons on remote controls. They're on the shelf next to the button on the wall."

Max looks at me blankly. He is not able to understand what I am saying to him, and he doesn't say anything in response.

"With a running start we can jump and hit the button, thus opening or shutting the garage door. Animals do not typically have this type of power. We could be the first. For some reason, the feline gods have only granted the power of technology to inferior humans."

"After all of the people are away from home, we will practice using the button. We can't let the people know we have this ability. Otherwise, the people could change the button that opens and shuts the garage door. Until the people leave, we need to do what we normally do, but once they leave for work and school, we will practice using that button."

I leave to take a nap in the sun, but it's hard to nap while I ponder all the possibilities of that button. Max has no problem doing what he normally does. He's too absentminded to think about important things like implementing technology to exert advantage over others. Max chases bugs and butterflies. The garage door has been open all day because the people have been getting things in and out of the garage periodically for sports and working in the yard. I do appreciate how they keep my yard nice.

I doze off, and when I wake up, I don't see Max.

Where has Max gone to?

I bet he went to go do something foolish with the garage door opener before my people have left. I rush over to the garage, I enter it, and I see Max on top of the large portable heater. He's playfully batting at something. He's toying with the handle attached to the garage door opener inside of the garage. It hangs from a rope about one-foot long.

I think to myself how I'm going to scold Max: *What are you doing? Can't you wait until the people leave? They all leave together to go eat at a restaurant on this day. You could have ruined everything by not waiting.*

"Max!" I call out to scold him. I startle him, and he leaps off the top of the portable heater. His paw gets caught on the handle that hangs from the garage door opener.

I hear a clicking noise, and then Max falls to the ground.

"What is that thing you're messing with?" I ask. "It's connected to the garage door opener, you know?"

"I don't know," Max says. "I was just playing, and it was hanging there, moving just a little bit, and I couldn't control myself. I'm sorry."

"I hope for your sake you didn't break it."

That evening, like always on this day of the week, all of my people get into the portable heater to drive someplace else for dinner. One of the big people had to spank one of the children for not getting into the portable heater. I sit in front of the garage as they drives away. I hear the familiar grinding of the garage door opener behind me that I've heard most of my life.

However, a second after the familiar sound starts, a loud

clank makes me instinctively jump away. The metallic sound reverberates throughout my domain, and all of my fur sticks straight out. The heavy metal garage door has slammed down. I look back to my people's portable heater on the street, but it's already driven away. The slamming door had narrowly missed me.

I'm furious at Max.

I know when he was messing around with the handle that he did something to the garage door opener. I rush around to the other side of the garage so that I can enter through the cat door into the garage. Max is already inside.

"You had better hope that when you messed around with the garage door opener, you didn't break it."

Max doesn't say anything, but I can tell he feels bad by the way he's looking down at the ground. He won't look me in the eyes. I can't waste time venting my anger on Max now.

"Let's practice running, jumping, and then pressing the button with our paws," I say. "It will be hard, but with practice, we can do it. I'll go first."

I run, leap, and extend my paw to press the button, but I miss. After two more tries, I hit the button. I'm relieved when the garage door cranks open. Max tries as well, but after six attempts, he's too tired to get anywhere near the button.

"Let's push something over here like a broom that we could lean against the button to press it," I suggest. We make a mess of the garage, rearranging all of the brooms, snow shovels, and skis so that we can get them near the garage door button. None of them work.

We even try rolling the children's red wagon under the button and tilting the handle over to hit it. We discover it doesn't reach nearly high enough.

I know the people will return imminently, and so I must conceal our activities.

"Play like a crazy kitten," I tell Max, "so that when the people come home they won't suspect anything about the garage door opener and all the stuff we rearranged." Max is happy to listen to that command, and so he makes an even bigger mess in the garage. The people won't be mad at Max for making a mess.

After several more leaps, I hit the garage door button again, and it shuts. It looks like Max didn't break the garage door after all. Pressing the button got the garage door opener back on track. The handle Max pulled on accident must have released the door from its track.

"Don't tell anybody about our secret," I warn Max before my people arrive home. Max gives a nod and sticks his chest out. He's proud to know my secret, and he's given me his trust in exchange.

There are other things I need to teach Max—things I need to warn Max about. Otherwise, he will run out of his nine lives before he is useful to me.

16

The next day, I sneak with Max into one of the neighbors' garage. This neighbor, who lives diagonally behind my house, does not have any pets. Max nearly falls off the fence on our way because he's so clumsy. I'm sure the people who live in the house will chase us away once they see Max intruding. These people do not like animals. Not at all.

A small opening allows me—and anybody smaller—to enter their garage. The people have assumed that putting some rocks in front of the hole would prevent animals from entering. This house is the worst in my domain. The people don't take care of this house. I'm bringing Max here because there's something I want to show him: mousetraps.

Max needs to be aware of the things people put in their yard and house that I have no control over. He has to learn these things to help me rule my domain.

"Not all people are as wealthy, famous, or powerful as our

family," I tell Max, "and so not all people have cats. These people don't have any animals, which shows they were at least smart enough not to get a dog."

"Why do we have to be so quiet and careful?" Max inquires.

"The people who live here are crazy," I say. "If they see us, they will attack us and chase us away. I need to show you what a mousetrap is. Because they don't have any pets, mice feel free to move in."

We maneuver around the pile of rocks that conceals the hole that leads us into the garage. I find several mouse traps lining the interior wall of the garage.

"Do you see these mousetraps?" I ask. "These can be incredibly painful if you try to take the bait. It could ruin your paw. Only a cat as strong as Patches should mess with such things. Be careful and stay away."

I inspect one of the traps, being careful not to get too close. The trap has old bait on it. These people haven't had mice in a long time.

I notice that Max is looking at something in the air, and I follow his eyes. Max is looking at a spider climbing in its web in an upper corner of the garage.

SNAP!

The crack of metal striking wood splits the silence of the garage. Max leaps into the air with a shriek.

Max inadvertently set off one of the mousetraps. When Max lands on the ground, he's still shrieking in pain, and I see a mousetrap latched onto his tail. Max must have been twitching his tail while watching the spider, which set it off.

Max races around the garage, doing anything he can to get the trap off his tail. During his rampage, he sets off more traps. He thrashes around the garage like a cat trapped in a vat of water. He bashes into everything, knocking things over in all directions. Bottles, jars, and old sports equipment tumble off shelves.

Max unleashes his signature pathetic meow intermixed with his howls, begging for help. I rush out of the garage. I look back and see the neighbor lady person burst out of her house and open the garage door. She wields a broom. Max finds his way out of the garage, but the mousetrap still clings to his tail. Some of the cans and bottles have toppled on to Max. Motor oil, green paint, and who knows what else, now color his fur. Sawdust, old cobwebs, and pieces of trash then affix themselves to his previously orange coat.

The woman person waves her broom at Max, but she can't hit him. She whips Max into more of a frenzy. The big neighbor lady person begins to sneeze in rapid succession while her face turns red. I don't think she can see very well. She hacks and coughs. Just when I think she is about to somehow hurl a fur ball out of her mouth, the woman rushes back into her house. Max finds his way and stumbles out of her yard and into Chief's yard.

Max and I go back to our house separately after Chief helps Max remove the mousetrap. In my house I act like nothing happened, but the small children people are full of mercy and compassion for Max.

Do they not realize that this only encourages Max to be more of a buffoon? I ask myself.

I'm glad I didn't get messy like Max, because later that night the people give Max a bath. I can smell the stinky chemicals all the way at the other end of the house. Most cats would hate getting wet like this, but Max enjoys the attention. Later that day, the woman from the house who tried to batter Max with a broom—I had secretly hoped that she would find her mark—comes over to talk to the big people in my house.

"I can't believe what happened in my house earlier today!" the woman says breathlessly.

"What happened?" asks my big man person.

"Some beast, maybe a possum, or raccoon, found its way into my garage, and it made the most horrendous mess," the woman says. "I was allergic to it. When I went after it with my broom, my eyes closed shut, my face turned red, my skin started itching, and I started coughing uncontrollably. I had to run back into the house."

My big man and woman person look at each other instead of looking at the neighbor woman as she speaks.

"Yes, maybe it was a possum, or a raccoon," says my big woman person tentatively.

"I already have mousetraps, and rat traps, and now I guess I'll have to get a bigger trap," says the neighbor woman. "I thought I should let you know to be on the lookout for possums or raccoons."

"Thanks for the tip," says my big man person. "We will be on the lookout."

As soon as the woman goes back home, my big man person says to my big woman person, "It's probably a good thing we didn't tell her that Max came home covered in paint that matches her kitchen."

17

A few days later I slink around my domain to check on everybody. Nobody knows that I'm watching, but I always am, and I always know what's happening in my domain. I see the bunny rabbits, the mice, the squirrels, and the birds. There are no animals in my domain who are not under my control. However, as I approach the neighbor's yard where the mousetrap caught Max, things seem a little bit different. It's quiet. None of the smaller animals are playing. Even though they are not as smart as me, all of the other animals do have their own sensibilities.

Something is ... *off*.

I head over to the yard that is directly next to mine so that I can talk to Chief about it. I hop up onto the fence overlooking Chief's pen.

"Does anything seem odd to you?" I ask.

"None of my paws hurt bad," says Chief. After a short pause, he adds, "But you're right. Something does seem a little hinky."

"You know anything about it?"

"I did hear the people from over yonder, the ones who tried to beat Max with a broom, talking earlier today."

I sit perfectly still as if I already know everything that Chief is going to tell me.

"A man and a woman person at the house were talking, and they said something about 'Animal Control.'"

All animals know the legend of Animal Control. I, and other animals like Chief, have people in our house, or we live in the people's house. Either way, if people live in your house, or you live in a person's house, Animal Control will leave you alone. However, some animals, especially skunks, occasionally get in trouble with Animal Control. Nobody is sure exactly who Animal Control is, or what they do. All we know is that once Animal Control takes somebody away, you never see them again, and you never hear from them again. There are legends of animals being taken by Animal Control, and then coming up later, but in all those cases, the animals have gone loony.

I need to go investigate. I can't trust Max to handle this. He still has some of the neighbor's dried paint on his fur, and I can't allow them to see that. I need to go check myself.

"What do you think is so hinky over there?"

"The only thing over there is what you take with you," Chief says.

Chief is getting batty in his old age, I think to myself.

I quietly pad over to the neighbor's yard, and it doesn't take long to find out what's different. Next to the garage is a wire cage. It's plenty big for me to fit inside of it. It's too small for Chief, though. There's also a pile of fruit inside the cage. I know exactly what this is.

It's a trap.

But it's too large for a mouse or anything like that. It must be a trap for what I heard those people talk about: possum, or raccoon. I hurry back to Chief.

"Tell me about a possum or raccoon," I say to Chief.

"Raccoons have not been around here in ages," says Chief. "But during Patches' time, may he rest in peace, there were possum. And I've seen them on television, too." I sit stiffly silent, pretending I already know everything that he's going to tell me.

"Possums are nasty creatures," says Chief. "They waddle around, they have little snouts and beady black eyes, and they hiss and snarl. They're hardly afraid of anything, except they play dead if they ever do get afraid."

I can't imagine what this possum animal is like if Chief describes it as nasty. Dogs don't think hardly anything is nasty; they sometimes eat their own poop, after all.

Max pops up onto the fence next to me.

"Ooh, ooh," says Max. "Tell me more about possums. I love learning about other animals."

Chief is about to answer, but both me and Max spot something amiss in the neighbor's yard. I sense it, and Max senses it too. It's more than the trap. It's alive.

It's a legendary beast that has never entered my domain before.

It's the serpent.

"What is it?" Max asks.

"It's a snake," I say, simplifying for Max.

"Is a snake good or bad?"

"Snakes are not good or bad, but they always bring bad things with them."

I can see the tiny wheels turning inside of Max's head, but I know he doesn't understand.

"Never, ever trust a snake," I say. "Snakes are incredibly self-centered, narcissistic, self-indulgent, and they always lie."

"Oh, kind of like—"

"Like what?" I say.

"Never mind..." Max says.

"I need to go confront the snake," I say. "You must not come with me. Stay away. You must not listen to the snake. You must never talk to the snake. Understand?"

"Okay, sure," says Max.

I stare Max down for another few seconds just to make sure he understands what I have told him.

I make my way over to the snake to confront it.

18

I hop up onto the top of the fence where I can look down on the snake. It is barely visible amongst the brush.

Excellent camouflage, I think to myself. I recognize this is no regular snake. It's a rattlesnake.

"Do you think you could enter my domain," I call out, "without my notice? Have you not heard of me—Princess?"

No response comes.

"Answer, or you will not be welcome in my domain," I say.

Still no answer.

"Do not test me," I say. "I wield the power of Animal Control." This is not completely true. I'm confident I could concoct some way to get my people to call Animal Control, but I don't really want to do that. Animal Control would definitely get the rattlesnake out of my domain, though.

The snake finally speaks.

"I'm sorry," comes the hissing voice. "I was so struck by the beauty of your majestic kingdom." It sounds to me that the snake is a female. Maybe she will understand along with me how hard it can be to be a lady in an animal's world.

"State your business, snake."

"My business is my own ... *hissss.*"

"In my domain, everybody's business is my business. Now tell me."

"I have been sent away from my previous home. Others have taken all of my food. Surely there is plenty within your kingdom."

"Who could take away your food?"

"Snarl, that nasty coyote, is raising an army that consumes all the small game in my former home," answers the snake. "I've come here seeking more food. Surely your domain is rich with small animals, and your people would surely appreciate some-body who can get rid of what they would call vermin ... *hissss.*"

"You think I cannot handle the vermin?" I ask incredulously.

"Just that your domain is so abundant," answers the snake.

To my surprise, Max jumps up onto the fence, and says, "Did you say Snarl is raising an army?"

I smack my paw against my forehead, angered by Max's disobedience.

"I said, 'Don't say a word to that snake,'" I admonish Max under my breath.

The snake doesn't answer the question about Snarl. Instead, she locks eyes with Max.

"Did she really say that you should not talk to me?" says the snake.

"She said I could watch and listen, but I should not be seen or even speak a word," Max says.

"She knows I can tell you of things that she does not know,

things she would like to know. Would you want to be like Princess?" asks the snake.

I'm a little bit thrown off by this flattery, and I see Max crouch to leap off the fence towards the rattlesnake. Max gazes into her eyes.

I let out a ferocious hiss and leap at Max. I grab him by the scruff of the neck and pull him away.

The rattlesnake settles down, and lowers its head from striking distance. I hadn't noticed—and I'm sure Max hadn't noticed—that the rattlesnake's head had been poised to strike.

I take Max back to my yard for scolding, but Max is so mesmerized, he even talks about going back to talk to that snake more.

"Our true enemy is Snarl, and now we know that he intends to wage war with an army of coyotes," I say.

That is what we must focus on now.

19

"**F**inding this magical animal is the key to defeating Snarl," I tell Max after I have some time to think following my encounter with the rattlesnake.

"Tell me more," Max begs as I describe the fantastical beast to him.

In addition to all of the normal activity, there is a lot going on in my domain: a rattlesnake has moved in, and the neighbor put in a possum trap. To distract Max, I've decided I need to send him on a special mission. I'm sending Max to hunt the magical, and non-existent, jackalope. It will keep him out of my luxurious gray tabby fur for a little bit.

"The jackalope looks like a giant jackrabbit, except that he has antlers like a deer," I tell Max.

"How can he help us defeat Snarl?" he asks.

"Jackalopes are incredibly rare, but they have magical powers that can defeat even the worst of enemies, in ways that we don't understand. The trick is to catch him first. If you catch a jackalope, then he will have to let us use his powers to defeat Snarl in order for us to let him go."

"But if a jackalope has powers that can defeat Snarl, how could I ever catch him?" asks Max. Max is getting a little too smart for his own good. "And why can't he get away from us with his powers once we catch him?"

"It's magic," I say, hoping he doesn't ask more. "We can't understand it. Jackalopes are too wary of me, and I will never catch one. You, however, are new, and so you still have hope of catching one. Now, be off, and hunt jackalope tonight!"

Max bounds off into the night. I'm sure he will probably be distracted by a blade of grass and forget all about the jackalope.

I take it easy tonight. I check on the snake and the possum trap, but neither has moved or caught anything since I last saw them. As I'm making the rounds, I run into Max, asleep on the fence. From his vantage point, he can see into a neighbor's house. Max was watching the pictures on the people's TV. I give him a rude shove to wake him up, half hoping he falls off the fence when he's startled out of his sleep.

"Hey! What's going on?" Max asks as he looks around to get his bearings.

I give him my steely glare.

"I was watching a TV show my old people used to watch," Max explains. "It's called the Johnny Carson Show, and he has this really happy guy bring lots of different animals for them to look at and make jokes about, and I guess I fell asleep, and you should have seen some of these animals..."

Max goes on and on about this TV show and the animals on it, and I keep expecting him to pause so that I can scold him, but he just keeps going. The third time he starts to tell me about the anteater, I decide something is seriously amiss. I've seen this before with kittens.

"Did you eat something?" I butt in.

"Like, what do you mean?"

"Catnip?"

"You got me. I chewed some catnip, but only to help my self esteem, and then I watched this TV show, and then I just totally fell asleep, and then... I totally forgot! I had a dream!"

I roll my eyes as Max continues.

"I know how to defeat Snarl," Max proudly announces.

"So you found a jackalope?" I ask, wondering what the catnip has done to him.

"I talked to a jackalope," Max says. At this point, I know that Max isn't really worth listening to.

Somebody calls to me from the front yard with a raised whisper: "Princess ... Princess," interrupting my discussion. Max doesn't notice and continues talking.

"The jackalope told me that coyotes fear people because they have guns that can kill coyotes. But that's not the only reason coyotes fear people. They dread being run over by those giant portable heaters. The jackalope called them 'cars,' and he said that many coyotes have been killed by cars. Guns are almost never responsible for killing coyotes these days."

"*Hmmmm*," I respond as I shift my eyes to the noise in the front yard. I fear a coyote is visiting right now, and I can guess who it is.

"The jackalope told me two ways to kill Snarl: guns and cars!" Max says. But I barely hear him, because I've decided I need to approach whomever has come to the front yard.

I hop up on the fence that divides the front yard from the back yard. It is a coyote.

"I bring a message from Snarl," Buck says. One of his eyes is swollen shut, his fur is even more scruffy and mangy than normal, and he seems extra skinny.

"You will deliver no message from that vile beast until you tell me what you were doing in my people's garage a few days ago," I respond before he has a chance to say more.

"Snarl says—"

"Silence! I will not listen until you tell me what you were doing in my people's garage."

Buck blinks, and I think he can't decide between serving Snarl and betraying him by helping me.

"Fine," Buck says. "I was humiliated when I couldn't capture one of those kittens. I needed to prove my worth to Snarl, or I would be out of the pack. So I stole something from the garage."

"What did you steal from me?" I ask, rising up on the fence.

Buck backs away slightly. "I took the BB gun pistol. Snarl knows it's the only weapon you could wield against him."

This is bad news. I had never thought of using the BB gun before. Now that I know it's not an option, I'm more frustrated with myself.

"The BB gun is merely a toy the people use to amuse themselves. I doubt it even works. Tell Snarl he doesn't have the fiercest weapon we wield against him."

"Snarl demands that you hand over to him the twin kittens and Max. If you do so, he will allow to you to continue as his puppet ruler."

"Get lost," I say.

"Snarl is amassing an army of coyotes. The most brutal ever. You have seven nights to decide. Hand over the twin kittens with Max and live, or Snarl and his coyote army will ransack your domain. I will return each evening for your answer."

Buck trots away with a limp and his head down. Buck isn't happy with Snarl as his master, but I can't trust him. I would love to get rid of Tweedledee and Tweedledum since they are so disrespectful, but that would be too much of an affront to my domain. I've invested so much in Max already. I don't want to lose him now.

I wander around my domain the rest of the night, pondering my options while Max sleeps. The catnip must have worn him out.

20

I shake slightly as I wander around my domain tonight. I know I didn't chew any of that catnip from Max. This is the first time during my reign I'm not exactly sure what to do. Buck told me Snarl is amassing an army, and so it turns out that the snake was at least partially telling the truth. These are dark days, indeed, when the snake is telling the truth.

I can't withstand a whole army of coyotes. For years, the coyotes defeated themselves by infighting, and Snarl used all of his resources to keep himself in power. He was never strong enough to build a critical mass and form an army that could truly attack my domain.

I go to speak with my trusted adviser, Chief.

After I tell Chief all that has taken place, he confirms that such organization and power amongst coyotes is unprecedented.

"I can't believe coyotes stole a gun," Chief says. "Even if it is just a BB gun. They have an instinctive fear of guns dating back for centuries when people would shoot coyotes, and even wolves, the most legendary of enemies, to keep them away from their livestock."

"It is unbelievable," I affirm.

"You willing to give up the twins and Max to Snarl?" Chief asks.

"I would love to get rid of Tweedledee and Tweedledum. But honestly, I would hate to lose my investment in Max. I've taken him under my wing, for better or for worse. Besides, he's from my very own house, fool or not."

"But you would give up the twins, wouldn't you?" Chief asks.

"I can't let that happen in my domain, even if I would like to be rid of those twins."

Chief's face relaxes. He blinks his eyes.

"Do you see what's going on?" Chief asks.

I'm not sure what to say, and so I follow my instincts.

"Of course I know what's going on," I say, hoping he doesn't ask me to clarify.

"Max and the twins are easy prey for Snarl anyways," Chief says. "If you give up the twins or Max to Snarl, Snarl won't keep his word and leave you in power, even as his servant. Snarl would attack, and you would be known as the traitor who gave up her own subjects to a coyote. Your kingdom would crumble before Snarl's army ever attacked."

I take in a deep breath when I hear this, and I struggle to control my anger. The hair on my back sticks up. Who could think that I would be a traitor and an unjust ruler?

"Tell Max the truth," Chief says. "Then you can prepare. But, you need to tell Max the truth, that Snarl wanted you to hand Max over to him."

I ponder this for a few seconds before Chief speaks again.

"And don't forget about Buck. He may be an ally yet."

"Thanks, Chief," I say as I walk away. I'm going to leave Max out of this for now, and I need to figure out how I can get Buck on my side. If I let Max know all that is going on, he won't be able to handle it.

21

I have an idea the next day. While Max spends his time lazing around in the sun and playing with bugs, I busy myself in the neighbor's yard where Max had previously been bathed in paint and motor oil.

Luckily, Max is preoccupied with playing his silly games and looking for catnip, and so I am able to gather all the materials I need for my plan. I gather leaves, tree bark, and sticks. I haul this all over to the neighbor's garage and place it next to the possum trap. I then rearrange all of the materials to disguise the possum trap. Night falls just as I finish. It looks like a pile of random yard waste that could be found in the corner of anyone's unkempt yard. Now I just need to find one last thing for the trap, and I will have Buck as an ally for sure.

I spend the next twenty minutes hunting for a mouse. Along the way, I see Max jumping at butterflies fluttering just out of his reach. I don't understand how he can enjoy himself when there is so much imminent danger. He is obviously not ready to rule his own domain, let alone be a trusted vassal in mine. It doesn't take long to catch a mouse, and I carry it back to the possum trap without anybody noticing.

It's tricky, but I manage to drop the dead mouse through the wire roof of the possum trap. It lands next to the fruit bait without setting the trap off. This will work perfectly to capture Buck. I go to my front yard, and when dusk falls, I see Buck approaching from afar. I climb up onto the fence where he can't reach me. When he's near, I say, "Meet me by that neighbor's garage," and I head off to the possum trap.

As I hurry back to the possum trap, I look over my shoulder to see if Buck is going to make his way around the block to the neighbor's garage. I'm happy to see that he is finding his way, and will soon be joining me. However, when I get to the possum trap, guess who I see sitting inside the trap.

Of course, it's Max.

Thankfully, he has the presence of mind not to let out his pathetic meow. I get closer to scold him, and I realize why he hasn't let out his pathetic meow. He's still playing with the dead mouse I left as bait for Buck.

"You are going to be in trouble for this," I tell Max.

I don't have time to mess with Max right now. I rush to the front yard of the house to meet Buck before he arrives to see Max in a cage intended for him. I intercept Buck near a bush and say the first thing that comes to mind to divert him.

"Snarl needs to wait. The neighbors are going to get a new kitten soon. If Snarl waits, I can give him not only the twins and Max, but also this new kitten. Wouldn't that be better?"

"Another new kitten?" says Buck. "I will deliver your message to Snarl and return tomorrow night with his reply." He heads off to Snarl.

I return to the possum trap to see if I can free Max and then give him a piece of my mind. I find out, however, that he overheard my conversation with Buck.

"What was that about giving me and the twins to Snarl?"

Uh-oh, I think to myself.

"I had to lie to Buck," I explain. "I had to tell him something. I was just buying time." Max puts on an expression I can only describe as cautiously confused. After several attempts, I'm not able to get Max out of the possum trap, and so I have to leave him for the people when they wake up in the morning.

Max punishes the whole neighborhood with his obnoxious meows for help all night. The woman stumbles bleary eyed out of her house early in the morning. Red-faced and sneezing, she releases Max from the trap, but not without muttering insults at him. She resets the trap with fruit for a possum.

Buck returns the next night with a response from Snarl. Snarl will allow me one more week. After that, he demands the twins, Max, and yet another kitten—who doesn't really exist. No excuses.

22

A few days later, the big woman person of my family is talking on the telephone.

"Oh, I know, me too," she says. This is a typical conversation. People spend a lot of time talking to each other on the telephone, but they are never really saying anything. Almost all of what they say is just like that: "Oh, okay, I see." But then she says something that interests me.

"You almost ran over a *coyote* this morning?" she says as if a coyote were a jackalope. She nods her head and gives the typical, "Oh, okay," but I see her face grow longer. She is worried.

"There were how many of them? And they wouldn't move off the road?"

She listens for a few seconds.

"And then they just disappeared?"

She intersperses her listening with a few longer "ohs." Her mouth hangs open slightly.

"Maybe we should keep Max and Princess inside at night. It is always sad when a pet goes missing."

This confirms for me that Snarl is indeed amassing an army. People are reporting missing pets. Packs of coyotes are not afraid of cars; they won't get out of the way for them. I soon discover something that is much more concerning. Chief calls me over when I'm outside for a stroll.

"You need to go over to that neighbor's house with the possum trap," Chief advises. "I've been told by Mr. Robin that there is a message waiting for you in the front yard."

"A message?"

Chief blinks his eyes and nods slightly, and then he lowers his head back down as if he needs to take a nap. I know better than to ignore any of Chief's advice.

I walk to the neighbor's yard, but I don't see anything odd near the possum trap or in their backyard. I pass by the rattlesnake's new home, but she has been undisturbed for quite a while now. I can hardly tell if she's still around.

I hop up onto the neighbor's fence and look into the front yard. It doesn't take me long to find the message. It is the carcass of some animal. I get as close as I can along a fence railing, but I can't be sure exactly what the animal is. I look around warily, and I rotate my ears to be sure nothing waits in ambush. Detecting nothing, I dash over to the carcass. It is a dead cat about my size and age, with coyote bite marks. The victim must come from a domain far away because I do not recognize him, but Chief is right. This is a message from Snarl.

23

After I tell Max about the dead cat in the neighbor's front yard, he isn't willing to help me. I promise him he won't get hurt, and I offer catnip in exchange for help. Chief is right; I need Buck as an ally, to be my spy amongst the coyotes. I need to trap Buck in that possum trap so I can turn him to my side. He never made it to the possum trap before since Max got caught in it, so the plan can still work. But I need Max's help to pull it off.

I adjust the camouflage around the possum trap. I leave an area in the back of the possum trap between the dead leaves and bark so that Max can hide and look as if he is inside the trap, but he will really be on the outside of the back wall of the trap. I don't tell Max he is the bait for Buck to enter the trap.

Max and I catch a few more mice and other assorted vermin, and we place them inside the trap. I explain to Max what he has to do. All he has to do is sit quietly and act afraid. I don't think he will have to act because he will be genuinely terrified.

"Be sure you stay put," I say. "Buck has to think you are inside the cage. If you get scared and jump away, Buck will know that you are not really in the cage, and he won't go in to get you."

Max nods slowly.

We spend the rest of the day doing what cats do. I sleep, but only warily, because I need to watch Max's behavior to see if he acts normally. Not that Max ever acts normally, but you know what I mean. He plays with bugs under the lilac bush, he chases butterflies, and he meows after birds. (That is so embarrassing.) He must be trying to keep his mind off what is going to happen tonight with Buck.

Once night falls, the people decide to put us outside.

"Don't worry about it," the big man person says. "Max is too dumb to be curious enough to find out about coyotes. He'll stay in our backyard. Princess is too smart to get caught by coyotes. It's the mediocre cats that get in trouble. They're not smart enough to get away from coyotes, but they're not dumb enough just to stay where they're safe."

I have underestimated this big man person. He is perceptive and wise.

When Max and I arrive at the possum trap, I demonstrate hiding behind the back wall of the cage. He nods slowly, climbs behind the back of the cage, and I cover him with leaves and bark. I come around and look into the mouth of the cage. What I see delights me. There are several dead rodents in the cage, and just beyond that, I see Max curled up in a ball, shivering with fear. The wire on the cage is thin and dark enough that it's impossible to see that Max is not really inside the cage.

We don't have to wait long for Buck to show up.

"Max is inside that cage for you," I say, hoping Max doesn't leap out of fear. "I have also provided an offering of several mice and other rodents for Snarl and his pack." Surely Max realizes I am not telling Buck the truth. Even though I'm lying about paying homage to Snarl, I'm still disgusted with myself for doing so.

Buck hesitates at the entrance of the cage.

"What about the other cats?" Buck asks.

"I will give them to you after Max."

The cage tremors from Max's shaking. Buck still doesn't enter the cage. Just like he didn't want to take Tweedledum before, he doesn't want to take Max now.

"The rodents inside are extra tasty," I say to entice Buck to enter the trap.

Buck doesn't move. I had not planned on this.

I need him in that cage.

Buck is about to say something, perhaps about Max, but before he does, Max releases a frightened *meow* and leaps out of the camouflage. Buck is startled and confused, and so I give him a firm push into the cage.

Click. I lock the cage, and Buck is trapped

Max runs around in circles like he's covered in paint and motor oil again.

"Max!" I call out. "You're not inside the trap. You are safe."

Max stops and looks around. He realizes that I am telling the truth.

Turning to Buck, I say, "We need to talk. It's for your own good." Buck pushes against the wire walls of the cage, whimpering with fear.

Now that Buck is in the trap, I have one night to convince

Buck to work for me and against Snarl. Buck can't stay away any longer than tonight, or Snarl will suspect something.

24

—————

"I'm giving you the chance of a lifetime," I tell Buck. Buck shifts around inside the cage that barely contains him. "Snarl is a horrible and cruel master. Join me, and together we can defeat Snarl and make things right again."

"You don't realize how powerful Snarl is," Buck says.

"I know all about the army he is amassing," I assure him. "This is not news to me, and it does not frighten me. Join me, and you can join in the victory over Snarl and his army. If you refuse to join me, you will be defeated and ground into the dust like Snarl and his pathetic club of overzealous, flea-ridden scoundrels."

"You've never met the likes of One-Eyed Jack and his other nasty lieutenants," Buck says. "I can't join you. Snarl will win. It is only a matter of time."

"What then?" I say. "I have you trapped in a cage. Snarl will have you killed for this embarrassing failure. You can't really go back to him, can you?"

"Snarl trusts me. I'm his messenger. He will be angry with you for trapping me." Buck is defiant, but I see flashes of doubt in his eyes. It's not me he's trying to convince, but himself.

"You wish Snarl would come to rescue you, but Snarl is using you."

"And so what if he is using me?" Buck says. "At least I will get something in return, and coyotes will have the empire they deserve."

I doubt whether or not I will be able to turn Buck to my side.

I need a break from this. I'll let Buck sweat it out alone in the cage before I try again.

"Oh, wow," Max says with astonishment. "Did you see that?" I've forgotten that Max is even here. I look over, and Max is playing with some roly poly bugs. He is shocked when they roll up into little balls when scared. I shake my head. I'm stuck. I take a brisk walk around the yard. After a few steps, I see some movement in the grass.

The snake.

"Perhaps I can be of assistance," says the snake. I'm not sure if this is a genuine offer, but I am stuck. "I want to return to my own home, and I am getting tired of hiding in this yard. There is barely enough food, and it won't be long before the people find me and call Animal Control. Or worse, I will get run over by a car as I try to slither across their driveway... *sssss.*"

"What do you have in mind?" I ask.

"Give me a chance to talk to the young coyote," says the snake. "I am most persuasive. Max can't help you with this." I squint at the snake, and the snake's eyes are wide open, trying to look as innocent as possible. Snakes are self-centered, selfish, and never to be trusted. The time to turn Buck to my side is almost up, though. I don't have a better idea. She's definitely right about Max. It wouldn't hurt to let the snake talk to Buck.

"What will you say to Buck?" I ask.

"You will see," she says cryptically. "You and Max must go into hiding. You can listen, but you must not be seen."

I nod in agreement with the snake.

"I had better not regret this," I say to warn her. "Come on, Max." We hop up onto the fence and move away into hiding, but we remain in earshot.

25

"Hello. Do you know who I am?" the snake asks Buck. Even from up on the fence, I can see the fear in Buck's eyes. His eyes dart back and forth, and he only nods his head slightly.

"Do you know Snarl's girlfriend?" the snake asks.

"Yes," answers Buck. His eyes lock with the snake's eyes. "She is beautiful. She is the most wonderful, and most beautiful coyote in all of the world."

"Yes," the snake says. "I know her ... *sssss*" The snake's hypnotizing gaze holds Buck. His head mirrors her sways.

"I don't believe you," says Buck. He shakes his head and blinks his eyes to disengage from the snake's gaze. "How could a snake know so much about Snarl and his girlfriend?"

"Me and Jennifer, that's her name, you know, are good friends. You coyotes believe that Jennifer knows many things and that she is like an all powerful god." Buck nods eagerly, but then he catches himself, and stops nodding. "Me and Jennifer have gotten along very well as friends for a while. We are girls, after all, and in the wild, we need to stick together. You could say that we are BFFs."

"She's your friend?" asks Buck.

"Close friend. Did you ever wonder why Jennifer is the only girl coyote?" The snake pauses while Buck thinks with a furrowed brow, but the snake doesn't wait for him to respond. "She is highly desired because she is the only girl coyote, but it's all because of me. Jennifer betrayed all of her sisters and all other girl coyotes born after her to me."

I can't believe it. I have to give the snake credit for being so cunning, but I'm disgusted that this girl coyote would allow her sisters, and all other girl coyotes, to be eaten by a snake. As much as I despise coyotes, the thought of a snake systematically swallowing all the baby girl coyotes repulses me.

"I know a way for you to have Jennifer for yourself," says the snake. "But for that to happen, I must be able to go back to my home. I don't like living here in Princess' domain."

I scoff at this, I even let out a soft growl, and Buck is almost snapped out of the snake's trance, but he goes back into it as I quiet myself.

"I will only help you get Jennifer for your girlfriend if I am able to go back to my own home."

"We want the same thing, then?" asks Buck, hypnotized.

"That is right. I want to go back to my land, and you want Jennifer to be your girlfriend. For both of those things to happen, we need to get rid of Snarl. In order to get rid of Snarl, you must agree to turn against Snarl and betray him to me so that Princess and I can defeat him. The result is that you will be the new leader of the coyotes, Jennifer will be your girlfriend, and I will return to my own home in peace."

Buck doesn't respond for a second. He must be imagining his future with Jennifer. For the first time, I sense that Buck may turn against Snarl.

"Discover Snarl's plan of attack, and bring it to me."

Buck nods his head slightly.

"And I want you to bring back the BB gun pistol," says the snake.

Buck wavers at this.

"I can bring information, even information that will ensure your victory, but bringing the BB gun pistol is another matter."

"Think of how impressed Jennifer will be if you take—and even wield—the BB gun pistol not once, but twice," says the snake. Buck's mouth opens slightly; I bet in his tiny brain he imagines Jennifer adoring him. Buck is so pliable. He is almost as bad as Max.

"I will let you out of the cage," says the snake. "And I will send you back with many of these rodents in addition to the ones in the cage for Snarl. Tell Snarl that the kittens were not here. There is a delay because they were taken to the vet to make sure that they are healthy. However, this will only ensure that Snarl will receive healthy new kittens. Bring back the news of his attack plan, and bring back the BB gun pistol."

The snake eases the latch open on the cage, and Buck exits warily. He starts to trot off, hardly believing that he is out of the cage.

"One last thing, future ruler of the coyotes," says the snake. "Do not double-cross me. You would not live to tell about it … *sssss*"

26

Everything seems completely normal in my domain the next day. All of my subjects are unaware of what awaits them if I do not stop Snarl. Buck returns that evening.

Before I can ask Buck anything, he delivers a message from Snarl.

"Snarl is angry," he announces to me, and anybody else listening, "and he knows you are lying and stalling. Consequently, he will send one of his lieutenants each of the next three nights, beginning tomorrow night, to terrorize this domain."

It doesn't seem to me that Buck is on my side. At least he's alive. Buck continues with Snarl's pronouncement.

"On the first night—"

"I will come down from the fence and speak to you quietly," I say. "There's no reason for everybody to listen."

"Snarl says this message is for everybody in the domain,

and not just for you," says Buck. I've never seen Buck so certain of himself. Perhaps Snarl has full control of Buck.

"On the first night, tomorrow night, Snarl will send his first lieutenant: Captain One-Eyed Jack. He is a river-raiding pirate who controls the waterways for Snarl. Snarl has promised some landlubbers for him to snack on. After the three nights are completed, Snarl will launch his full-out attack, and he guarantees that nothing will be able to save you, Princess, or those who remain foolishly loyal to you and do not meet Snarl's demands. Those who wish to join Snarl's side need only hang a red thread out their window, out their burrow, out their tree, or out their door. This will signify their allegiance to Snarl, and Snarl guarantees their safety under his impending rule."

This catches me off guard, I have to admit.

Buck trots away without saying more. He still limps. I wonder if the snake heard this and what she thinks about Buck's allegiance.

This leaves me little time to make a plan. I'm not going to get that BB gun pistol back from Buck any time soon. How am I going to make good on any plan to defeat Snarl? The BB gun pistol was my only hope.

Max comes up to me.

"I thought Buck was on our team," Max says, more as a question than a statement. "We can hide in the garage."

"We can't hide in the garage forever," I say. "Besides, if the people forget to shut the garage door even one time at night, we would be done for. Snarl would have access to the garage, which leads to my whole house. Even if I, or you, were to use the secret button and shut the door, the door shuts slowly, and Snarl would have plenty of time to enter."

Heat wells up in my chest as I discuss this with Max. I'm

indignant that my domain could be lost. Snarl would ruin, eat, and maim all of the fair game in my domain. I can't stand the thought of that. Only I have the right to do what I will in my domain.

I spend the night racking my brain, trying to cook up a plan to defeat Snarl for when he makes his attack after the third night. I'm not even sure how we will survive his lieutenant coming tomorrow night, this Captain One-Eyed Jack.

I make some small talk with Chief, but he doesn't offer up any of his trademark wisdom. Max shows up at dawn, giddy, dusty, and slightly weird.

"Did you find more catnip?" I ask.

"Totally," says Max. He's walking around like he's on a cloud.

"Don't people realize that catnip should be illegal?"

Then I see something hanging from Max's mouth. It's a red thread, and it runs around his body. Max is playing with this red thread.

"Where did you get that?" I demand.

Who has pledged their allegiance to Snarl?

"I don't remember..." Max says, clearly sensing something is wrong. I suspect the red thread came from Tweedledee and Tweedledum.

What Max goes on to tell me sounds more like a weird dream he had at night, not something that really happened.

27

C aptain One-Eyed Jack attacks the following night.

Max and I hide in the garage. I hear the coyote bark and growl outside. He's laying down a challenge. I still haven't figured out how I can finally defeat Snarl. There's no way I can give my domain to that beast, but I'm not sure how to defeat him and show my strength to my subjects.

"Let's stay in here and wait," Max suggests. "Maybe if we wait it out, he will leave us alone. Would it be so bad if we live inside the garage at night and inside the people's house during the day?"

"*My* house, you mean," I correct Max. "And leave my domain to that monster? Inconceivable. I must face One-Eyed Jack tonight. If I can fight and survive one night, it will show my subjects that this is still my domain, and I will defend it."

I go to the cat door on the side of the garage, and I look back to Max. I hope it's not the last time I see the inside of my garage. I even have to admit I hope it's not the last time I see Max. Max is on top of one of the big mobile heaters and playing with that string and handle hanging down from the garage door opener. *Will he ever learn?*

"Don't play with that. That breaks the garage door opener, remember?" I remind Max. Max turns aside and pretends he's studying a spider web.

I go out the door, and I hear Max call after me.

"Should I come with you?" Max says. It's timid, and I know he's praying I will tell him to stay in the garage.

"Do not come with me," I call back. "Stop playing with that string!"

It's not hard to find One-Eyed Jack. He is now ravaging a nest of bunnies who live near the apple tree. The refuse from several overturned trash cans is strewn across multiple yards. One-Eyed Jack has been digging several holes. I can at least start a good fight with One-Eyed Jack. His size tells me he is no average coyote. I hop up onto the fence and I sneak over to where he is digging away at the bunnies' burrow.

I know this bunny rabbit family. I've even captured and played with many of their family for meals and for sport. I don't despise them, though. They know, and I know, that they must pay at least ten percent tribute to me. That may include their offspring and their well being. Now it is my turn to fulfill my duty as lord over my domain. I must protect them from this horrific coyote. Coyotes would not accept ten percent like I do. They would wipe all of them out.

One-Eyed Jack is larger and smells worse than the average coyote. His fur is black with faint gray and white stripes, but his body is marked with large scars. He is the coyote version of a tiger, but with different colors. His ears, torn from previous fights, flop from side to side. An eye patch conceals one eye, and the other yellow eye scans his surroundings. He truly is a pirate coyote, and a successful one at that. His success has expanded his girth.

I know exactly what I need to do. I need to execute 'The Guillotine.'

I jump down from the fence onto One-Eyed Jack's back as he burrows into the bunnies' home. I do exactly what I taught Max to do. I bite into the scruff of his neck, and I start clawing furiously with my rear claws. One-Eyed Jack leaps into the air and twists around, yelping in pain and surprise. One-Eyed Jack's maneuver flings me from his back. He dashes at me with spit flying from his jowls. He snaps at my heels as the chase begins, but he trips me up.

I make myself into a ball and send my claws flailing every way possible. One-Eyed Jack has caught me by the leg, and a sharp pain runs up my body. It's only by a stroke of good luck that my front paw slashes his one good eye. His grip loosens enough for me to escape, and I go hobbling as fast as I can on three good legs. My fourth leg throbs with pain as I race away.

It's time for me to execute the most important part of my plan. I make it as quickly as I can to the neighbor's chain-link fence. One-Eyed Jack is close behind. I look back to see his one red eye bearing down on me.

I sneak under the chain-link fence as best as I can, and then I hop up onto the fence directly above the hole. I barely make the leap with the strength of three legs. The hole is the perfect size for me, but I know it will be too small for One-Eyed Jack. He shows that he is vicious, but he's not as smart as Snarl. He lunges into the hole, and his head sticks out on the other side. I look down at him.

One-Eyed Jack's head is stuck, but I know it will only last a few seconds. I leap down from the fence and claw and bite as viciously as I can at One-Eyed Jack. I want to make sure his name will become *No*-Eyed Jack. After a few seconds of fierce clawing, One-Eyed Jack pulls his head out of the hole, and he goes yelping in retreat. I follow him to the edge of my people's yard to make sure that he is gone for the night. I watch until he's out of sight, afraid he might regroup and come back. I look down and see his eye patch in my front paw. I drop it on to some nearby trash that One-Eyed Jack spread about my yard.

I limp back to the garage. When I get there, Max is waiting outside the cat door on the side of the garage. He's meowing helplessly, hoping against hope that the people would come out, or do something to get rid of the scourge of coyotes. My people have turned their lights on, but now that the commotion is over and One-Eyed Jack is gone, the lights are soon turned off. I go into the garage with Max, and I lick my wounds. I can't reach some of the cuts on my back, and so I reluctantly allow Max to lick those for me.

My people can't know that I'm injured. I can't afford a trip to the vet. A trip to the vet is horrible anyways, but I can't abandon my subjects at a time like this. I must remain here to defend my domain. I only have two more nights to withstand attacks from Snarl's lieutenants, and I only have two more nights to concoct a plan to defeat Snarl. But once I do, Snarl will be no more terrifying than the refuse from my litter box.

28

I spend the next day recovering from my injuries. I sleep
very little, which is unusual for me. At dusk, I sense Buck
lurking around the front yard of my people's house. I go
to look, but I'm not sure it's him until he peeks his head out
above a bush. We make eye contact. He's not trying to hide from
me, and I hope he has a message. I can't let Buck see my injured
leg, even though it's not as bad as I originally thought. I still do
have a limp, though.

I need Max's help.

"Max," I call out. Max trots to my side.

"Yup?" Max says. He's incredibly upbeat and optimistic,
seemingly unaware of the danger that surrounds us the next
few nights.

"I need your help. I have a mission for you."

Max gives me a slightly confused look, as if I must be
making a mistake.

"Buck is on the edge of my yard," I tell Max, "and you need

to go find out what Buck wants. Report back to me. He may have a message to help us defeat Snarl. However, if Buck is not here to help, then this is a perfect chance for you to practice The Guillotine."

"Why am I going alone? Why don't you go? Why am I supposed to be either friendly or fight with Buck?" I take a second to think before I explain this to Max in the simplest terms possible, but Max comes up with an idea before I can.

"Are you actually sending me on a jackalope hunt?" Max says.

"I have some catnip for you if you bring back a report," I say, having decided that a simple bribe is the easiest way to go.

Max leaves without hesitation. I watch Max, and I can't help but shake my head when a butterfly distracts him and he swats at it. Fortunately, Max continues on, and I watch him until he's out of my sight.

I don't hear any meowing or yelping, and so I guess Buck is friendly with Max. Max returns a few minutes later, but it feels like an hour.

"I got confused trying to convince Buck to let me ride him like a horse so that I could fight him and scratch him. Buck didn't want to play horsey," Max reports.

"What did Buck say?" I ask.

"Buck wouldn't play horsey, and he said a different coyote will come tonight with his apprentice. This coyote, he said, is wicked evil, and he's rumored to be part wolf. His apprentice is part wolf as well. He's huge and fat. He's known as *Killer*. Buck told us so that we could warn everybody and stay inside tonight." I shake my head in disgust. This is just unnatural. Coyotes who exert authority over any domain, especially *my* domain, infuriate me.

I don't think Buck is lying about Killer, and so I decide to stay in and wait to face Snarl the following night.

I just hope I can survive this night.

"What will you tell everybody?" says Max.

This could be the smartest question Max has ever asked.

I must make a speech to address the subjects of my domain. I must convince them to wait one more night, and then I will give them victory and salvation from Snarl.

"Have you seen any red thread today?" I ask.

Max looks at me with confusion, obviously unsure of what the red thread means.

"Oh, it is all over the place outside, and it sure is fun to play with," Max says.

I only have a few more hours before the people go to sleep and Killer shows up. I need a Winston Churchill-like speech to exhort my subjects to remain strong for one more night.

29

It is time for me to address my domain. I am their empress, and I must encourage them in the face of the onslaught that will come from this coyote-wolf thing called Killer. I can't allow them to see how badly I'm injured, or they may lose courage. One-Eyed Jack dealt a wound to me, but that won't stop me from building the confidence of my subjects. I glance around the garage, and I get an idea from the red wagon.

"Max," I say, "you're going to wheel me out into the yard so that I can give a speech to my domain."

"Why do I have to push you in the red wagon?" says Max.

"I will look more regal that way. I will look more like an empress." I emphasize the last word to impress Max.

"Well, okay, whatever you say."

I hop up into the wagon with a wince. I look around the garage for something inconspicuous to cover my other injuries. Max senses something is wrong.

"What's the matter, Princess?" says Max.

"I need something that reminds my domain that I am their empress. Go and search the garage. Find something that makes me look like an empress."

Max rummages through boxes, around old cans of paint, and even behind the snow shovel that leans unused in the corner.

"You know what an empress is, don't you?" I say.

Max freezes and looks at me, and he doesn't say anything for a second. I'm afraid that Max has no idea what an empress is, and so he doesn't know what he's looking for.

"An empress looks like you," he says. "You're an empress." He's right, but of course, even a blind cat catches a mouse now and then.

"An empress," I explain, "is like a very powerful queen who rules not only her own country, but over many countries."

"So you are an empress," Max says.

He's starting to get the idea.

After searching another minute, Max finds an old costume that one of the children had worn last year. People have this strange tradition of sending their children around the neighborhood when it starts to get cold outside to collect candy from all their neighbors. They demean their children by forcing them to dress up as odd things. My people were kind to their children, and they allowed one of them to dress up as a superhero. Oddly, he wore colored underwear on the outside of his pants. I'm not sure why superheroes do that. Max has found that costume.

The costume is red and blue, and I remember that there was something that he wore on his shoulders, something that was called the "cape." I remember the boy child would run around and say that he was "Wonderman."

"Bring the cape to me," I command. Max brings the cape to the wagon, jumps up, and drapes the cape onto my back. It covers most of my body, especially my hindquarters. The cape matches nicely with the red wagon, it hides my injuries, and I look exactly like an empress who is needed to defend her domain. The red color reminds me we are going to war with Snarl.

30

I ride in my new chariot, the red wagon, to my backyard. Instead of stallions pulling my chariot, I have Max. He will have to do for now.

The wagon's squeaky wheels are all I hear in the midst of the silence. Everybody knows something is about to happen, even if they don't know exactly what. Max pulls the wagon near the woodpile, and I jump out with three good legs. I pick my way up the woodpile to the top of the fence. The cape hides my limp and other injuries. I look out over my domain from atop my perch. A slight breeze comes up, and my cape flaps in the air. I'm worried it will show my injuries, but then I realize it displays my majesty.

I look around to make sure everybody is listening. Chief stands up on his hind legs and puts his front legs on the fence. He gives one friendly bark. Then he lies back down like he normally does with his chin flat on the ground. This is a friendly show of support, and it makes sure that everybody will be listening to me. I look up, and I see the robins gathered in the trees, all of them lined up on the branch to listen to what I have to say. The bunnies huddle under a nearby lilac bush. I think I smell the skunk, but I don't want to make certain. I see other birds and other wildlife, and even the snake must be listening to what I have to say. It is time for me to address my domain.

I lift my voice and say: "My subjects and my friends, dark days are upon us. Snarl the coyote is a cruel enemy, and he will show you, your families, and all of your friends, no mercy. It is true, as you have heard, that Snarl has given me mere days to surrender some of my subjects to him. Doing so would make their death certain by horrible and wretched means. In return, Snarl promises he will allow me to rule as one of his vassals under his power.

"But he lies. He would take the subjects of my domain, but he would not keep his promise. Then, he would continue to attack my domain. He would steal your children. He would kill your friends and family. He would wipe them out. All of them.

"Tonight, one of his lieutenants, Killer, will attack and ravage my domain. Do not fear; his new name will soon be: 'Defeated by the Mighty Princess.'

"On the next night, Snarl himself will attack. We must wait and survive tonight, but I promise salvation will come. Survive one more night, and I promise that tomorrow night, I will defeat Snarl when he launches his final assault on my domain. I refuse to give my subjects to him, and I refuse to make any treaty with him. Snarl's name will be forgotten, and Killer will be renamed, if you just wait for one more night."

I pause and look around to see how my subjects are reacting to my speech. Should I mention the red threads? I do see a red thread lying on the ground. It was previously part of somebody's home, but I don't know whose. I suspect Tweedledee and Tweedledum are to blame. Others in my domain follow the gaze of my eyes to the red thread, and I'm about to declare a denunciation of any traitors who have displayed red threads. Traitors deserve to be punished.

But then I hear a bump from the fence near Chief's pen. Chief gives a light cough. I look over at Chief, and I can see one of his pleading eyes through the crack in the fence. He must know what I'm thinking, and he wants me to forget this red thread, just this one time. I know Chief is right.

But then the jeers and taunts come from my very own subjects.

"We can't go hide in the people's garage like you," somebody calls out.

"That's right!" others yell in agreement.

"Snarl's Lieutenant, Killer, may not be able to get to you in the garage, but we will be exposed to him for this one night. You ask us to wait it out one more night while you sleep in safety?" somebody calls out in anger.

Heat swells up in me to meet the challenge.

One other voice rises from the quarreling, and it comes from one of my meeker subjects. It is the bunny rabbit.

"She attacked One-Eyed Jack last night," says the bunny rabbit. "She didn't have to. She could've waited in her garage, but she didn't. She attacked One-Eyed Jack at great risk to herself," says the bunny rabbit. "Princess our queen, aye, our *empress*, risked her very own life for my children who were hiding in our burrow from One-Eyed Jack. Because of that, I owe her my allegiance, my trust, and so when she says we must wait one more night for salvation, I will trust her and wait one more night."

A note of support is the perfect way to end my speech. I hop down from the fence onto the woodpile and back into the wagon, hiding my limp. I feel the gazes of my subjects, and some must suspect I'm injured worse than I let on.

There is a murmur in the crowd. Some are still opposing me, but some are siding with the bunny rabbit and supporting me, even though I can't tell exactly what they are saying.

Max looks over at me and says quietly, "Great speech, Princess. That was really good." He looks down at the ground and asks nervously before pulling my wagon, "I can hide in the garage with you, right?"

"Just get moving," I say to Max. Max starts hauling the wagon once again with me in back towards the garage, and I continue to hear the jeers from some of my subjects. Nuts, small sticks, little vegetables, and perhaps even fruit, fly at me from the tree. This is the low point of my reign over my domain. Never before have any of my subjects been so bold as to throw things at me. Chief is right; I can't retaliate against them. That would only reveal my injuries. I'm starting to worry that my plan to get Snarl the next night won't work. But it must work. If my plan doesn't work, I can't rule over my domain. If I can't rule over my domain, I don't care whether I am dead or alive.

31

Max and I wait inside the garage. It's completely quiet as the hours pass by. Everybody in my domain is doing the best they can to hide. The normal nighttime sounds—a prowling skunk snapping a twig or the chirp of an insomniac bird—are absent. Even the crickets are silent. Normally, I would be doing my rounds, making sure everything is as it should be in my domain. But not tonight. Instead, I cower with Max inside my garage.

I lose track of how many hours have melted away, and I wonder if Killer is ever going to attack. Is he going to come in making as much noise as he can? Maybe he will enter my domain quietly, kill everybody else one by one, and then finally face me.

I've assumed Killer would come in with all fangs and claws blazing, but maybe he will attack quietly.

He may also face me first in a duel. That way, everybody in my domain would witness my defeat at the paws of Killer.

The hours drag on, and it can't be much longer until the sun comes up. Waiting is the worst part of battle.

I hear a noise from outside, but perhaps I'm imagining it. After a pause, I realize it's panting from outside the cat door on the side of the garage.

"Princess," Buck says, "I've got something to tell you. It's important." I hobble warily over to the entrance, but I dare not go outside. It could be a trap.

"What do you have to say?"

"He comes tonight," Buck says.

"What do you mean, 'He comes tonight'?" I say. "I already know Killer is coming tonight."

"No. *Snarl* is coming tonight. Snarl and Killer got into a fight, and Snarl decided he would come a night early, decimate you, and that would show his power and worthiness, even over Killer."

Snarl is coming tonight. It takes a second for that to settle into my mind.

"Do you understand me?" asks Buck.

"But it's already very late," I say. "It will be morning soon."

"He wants to make you as nervous as possible so you would anticipate your own demise. He will come," says Buck.

Buck scampers off. I go over to Max and explain the situation. Before I finish, Max shivers.

"Max," I say, "you only need to do one thing." Max nods his head slightly in fear. "After I leave to face Snarl, all you have to do is press the button and open the garage door like we practiced. Okay?"

Even Max grasps the gravity of the situation as he ponders the possibility of me going out to face Snarl on my own. He may never see me again.

"I will fight against Snarl and make him chase me around as much as I can," I explain doubtfully as I look down at my injured leg. "And then I will lead him here at just the right moment."

"Just the right moment for what?" asks Max.

"Just the right moment for the big man person to run Snarl over with his car when he backs out to go to work," I explain.

"Won't the big man person open the garage door anyways?" Max asks. "Why do I have to open it?"

"I need every second I can get, and I can't wait for the garage door to slowly open. The big man person will simply assume he forgot to shut it last night."

Before Max is able to point out flaws in my plan, I exit the cat door on the side of the garage, and I go to await Snarl. I won't be able to miss his foul stench. I look back inside the garage, and Max is curled up in a ball playing with my discarded cape. I hope he doesn't get too distracted by playing with that cape and forgets to open the garage door. I hope the big man person pulls the car out of my garage like he does every morning to go to work.

32

I trace the perimeter of my neighbors' houses warily to detect Snarl's attack. Red threads hang from bushes, trees, and burrows. I know Snarl will not honor them. I wince with each step as I try to conceal my limp from any of my subjects who are brave enough to watch. Even those cheeky twins, Tweedledee and Tweedledum, are nowhere to be found. Perhaps they discovered a way to stay inside their house tonight.

A faint rustle breaks the silence.

I freeze and twitch my ears to analyze the noise. It's just Chief shifting in his pen. Chief normally sleeps the whole night. He kneads his paws on the ground. I make my way over to Chief. This might be the first time in my life that I need encouragement. If anybody can give encouragement to me, Chief can. Chief might be the only one who can. I hop up onto the fence overlooking Chief's pen.

"You awake?" I ask. "Don't be nervous."

"I am," Chief says. "Awake and afraid. I'm old. I can't fend off a coyote like Snarl. He would make an example out of me."

"For the rest of my domain, you mean?"

"Of course," Chief says. "I'm the only dog in these parts. And if Snarl were to defeat me, that would show he's a coyote who is more powerful than a dog."

Chief droops his head and creakily paces around his pen. He's always claimed to have arthritis, but I know dogs make excuses for their inferiority. I must admit, though, Chief is an exceptionally good dog.

"I wish there was some way I knew Snarl would attack me first, and I would have to go alone..." Chief says. "Didn't you say salvation would come tomorrow night?"

"I did say that..."

I need to tell Chief the truth.

"I don't mean to scare you," I say as I lock eyes with Chief, "but Snarl is coming tonight." Chief's eyes, dimmed with age, now expand with fear. "But salvation will come tonight as well," I promise. "With Buck as an ally—like you suggested—Snarl loses the power of surprise."

"Oh, but what if Snarl attacks me first and makes an example out of me? Nobody would be impressed if he killed some bunnies first."

"I'll see how he attacks," I say. In reality, I'm not confident in my ability to spot Snarl's assault before it's too late.

"I just know he'll come for me first," Chief says. Chief paws the ground, and his eyes dart from side to side even though he couldn't spot a coyote until it was right in front of him.

So much for getting encouragement from Chief.

I feel sorry for Chief. He is one of my best subjects. I am his empress. He has given me some good advice over the years.

"Don't worry, Chief," I say. "I'll stand guard nearby. I have a plan that will destroy Snarl once and for all. He should be coming any minute now."

Chief conceals a slight smile, and I go off prowling, trying to spot signs of Snarl's attack. I stay near Chief's pen, mostly so that he knows that I'm nearby. The timing must be perfect for me to defeat Snarl, and the clock is ticking. I just don't know when it will reach zero.

33

I f one step of my plan is out of sync, I will become coyote food, and my domain will be ruined. I make a quick run around my house to make sure it will be perfect. Every morning, the big man person backs his car out of the garage to go to work. He doesn't look where he's going so early in the morning. Snarl must come before the big man person drives the car away to work. The sun will rise soon.

Is it possible that Buck lied? Perhaps he's just wrong.

I climb the willow tree to gain a higher vantage point. I wince, but I'm not as badly hurt as I originally thought. I scan over my domain, and many red threads taunt me as they wave in the breeze.

But then, I see Snarl.

Chief was right. Snarl goes directly at Chief's pen. Snarl is going to try to make an example of Chief first. Then he will attack others or draw me out to face him. I can't let Snarl reach Chief's pen.

I rush down the willow tree on my three good legs. As Snarl passes under the tree, I leap onto his back. Pain shoots through my injured leg when I land, and I go for the scruff of his neck with my jaws. I scratch furiously. Snarl rumbles on towards Chief's pen, treating me as a mere nuisance. We're close enough to Chief's pen that I can hear Chief's whimpers.

Snarl smells of rotten fish, much worse than a skunk. I gag as I dig my fangs into him. His hide is tougher than anything else I've ever attacked. It's like thick leather, and I can barely get a hold of him. My claws inflict almost no damage despite all my noise and fury.

Snarl twists sharply, and I fly off his back. I land on all fours (of course) between Snarl and Chief's pen. My injured leg throbs.

Snarl looks at me, and I look at him.

He bares his fangs. Drool drips from his jowls, nearly reaching the ground without breaking. Remembering Max, I do my best were-bear.

The time has come.

Snarl lunges at me. His jaws snap in the air, and I swipe once at Snarl with my front claws. Then I sprint away.

Adrenaline pumps through me as I run, dragging one lame leg behind me. I make it to the chain-link fence, and I slide through the same hole that trapped Captain One-Eyed Jack.

The trap doesn't fool Snarl.

Instead of going under the chain-link fence, Snarl does the impossible. He leaps and clears the fence with one bound.

No coyote should be able to do that.

I'm caught off guard by Snarl's agility, and I'm just able to escape past the rickety woodpile as Snarl crashes onto it. I look back, hoping to see the woodpile tumbling over with Snarl caught in an avalanche of firewood. But Snarl is as nimble as he is smelly. He must have only been on the woodpile for a split second before he leaped off it. In a flash, Snarl has cleared the fence and the woodpile, drawing closer to clamping down on me with his jaws.

I race towards the front of the house.

But I don't hear the car starting in the garage yet. The big man person usually has the car warming up by now.

Did I not hear the car start in all my excitement?

Surely it is time. Daylight is coming. I run around the house with Snarl close behind. I'm barely fast enough to keep my distance from him. I can hear his laughter as he chases me. I feel as if he could catch me any time. Is he toying with me like I do with a mouse? I make it around to the front of the house, and I see the garage door gaping open.

Thank the feline gods Max remembered to open the garage door!

I look back, expecting to see Snarl's bloodshot eyes bearing down on me, but I see something else.

One of the twins dashes in front of Snarl, trailing something … it's red thread!

The twins dart in and out of Snarl's path attempting to tangle him up in red thread. For once, their mischief is helpful. It slows Snarl enough for me to gain a few valuable seconds as I approach my garage.

But the large portable heater is not running. There is no sign that the big man person has come out. My plan depends upon the man starting his car and then pulling out of the garage at exactly 5 AM—just as he has done every single morning for the last seven years—and then running over Snarl in the process.

What is different this morning?

As I rush towards the garage, I know I only have one chance to survive. I need to get inside of that garage.

"Shut the garage door! Shut the garage door!" I call out to Max. I rush into the garage, and Max leaps to press the button.

His paw glances off the side of the button on his first attempt. I crouch to attempt myself, but my lame leg prevents me from even jumping inches off the ground. Max leaps again, and it looks like he hits the button.

Time seems to stop once Max hits the ground. But then the garage door starts to grind close. It is closing too slowly. Snarl will enter the garage long before the door closes.

What went wrong? Where is the big man person?

Oh no, I realize.

Snarl came a day early.

It's Sunday morning, not Monday morning. For some reason, the big man person doesn't go to work on Sunday.

I stand in the back of the garage with my fur puffed up and my claws and fangs bared. The garage door inches down and Max goes to cower on top of the car. I will make my last stand against Snarl.

I wait to make my suicide attack, but the garage door closes. Snarl didn't come in. Did he wait outside? Max and I look at each other.

"What's the problem?" says Max. "Where's Snarl?"

34

"This must be the end," I say. "All we can do is wait in the garage. The big man person was supposed to hit Snarl with his car when he backs out like he does every morning. But, as you can see, he didn't back out this morning because it's Sunday morning."

Click.

The garage door opener grinds its gears as it inches the door back up.

This is bad news.

I look up to the garage door button on the wall, but there's nobody around who could have touched it.

What happened?

I leap on top of one of the large portable heaters to get as high as I can. I expect to see Snarl gnashing his teeth, eager to get in.

Before the garage door is completely open, I see Snarl standing about fifteen feet away from the garage on the driveway. He doesn't rush in. Something is on the ground in front of him. It's a button for the garage door opener.

Buck must have taken it for Snarl. He not only took the BB gun pistol for Snarl, but he also took one of the garage door openers. Now Snarl can open and shut the garage door any time he wants. There's nothing I can do to stop Snarl. I can't even hide from him in my garage.

Snarl flashes his fangs and growls, relishing this moment. If I thought Snarl was capable of it, I would think he is smiling as he shows his yellowed fangs. He must be savoring the thought of rushing into the garage and consuming Max and I in a flurry of blood and fur.

Snarl unleashes a ferocious bark and dashes towards the garage. I'm frozen in fear, but Max, startled by the bark, leaps into the air. I cover my eyes out of shame.

I don't want to see what happens. I've surrendered myself to Snarl. I must go down with the ship, as I've heard people say. As the empress of my domain I will give myself up for having failed my subjects.

But then I look and see Max hanging from the cord on the garage door opener. His look says, "Oops. Sorry."

The fool has unwittingly opened the door for salvation!

Now I must shut *the door for salvation.*

I make one desperate leap, grimacing in pain as I launch off one bad foot, to press the garage door opener button on the wall.

I make it just in time and press the button.

The malfunctioning garage door ruthlessly swings down.

I hear the thud of metal hitting flesh, and a yelp is followed by silence.

Snarl is on the ground at the entrance of the garage, and the garage door is smashed into his skull. He never crossed the threshold of the garage. Max hangs from the cord attached to the garage door opener. He must sense my stare, and he lets go and falls to the ground—not quite landing on all four feet.

"I'm so sorry, Princess," Max says apologetically, not aware of what he's done. "You told me not to play with that cord, but I got so scared and I didn't know what to do, and I jumped off the car, and I wasn't thinking, and I grabbed it because I love playing with it, and I guess I pulled it."

I open my mouth, but nothing comes out for a few seconds. When I do say something, it's a lie.

"I'm glad I had that backup plan." I stare in unbelief at Snarl's lifeless body.

Blood oozes from Snarl's skull underneath the garage door.

Snarl's corpse lies in defeat.

35

I can't believe it. I defeated Snarl. I sit frozen, astonished by what has happened.

Max runs out the side door of the garage and races around my yard as if he's doing laps. Max sings: "Ding, dong, Snarl is dead! Ding, dong, Snarl is dead!"

I can't believe I'm alive and breathing.

A familiar gasping sound comes to me. It's Buck. He's come to the garage to see what happened. I drag myself with my front paws to talk to him.

"You didn't tell me you gave Snarl the garage door opener," I say. "You only told me you gave him the BB gun pistol." Buck shrinks under my glare as he looks past me to Snarl, who lays in the garage door opening.

"I had to do what I could to stay alive. I had to give Snarl something. I just, I just, wasn't sure what was going on." Buck continues to make more excuses before I cut in.

"I will let it pass on my day of victory," I say, "but you must promise me something. You must always be my spy amongst the coyotes. You will be my servant and my subject for the rest of your life. And one other thing. It's your job to go tell the coyotes that Snarl is defeated. Make sure they know Snarl was defeated in an amazing and gruesome manner. You take credit for it, and you will be their leader. If you ever betray me, then I will tell the coyotes the truth. Do you get the idea?"

Buck nods his head. He trots away with his tail in between his legs to deliver the news to the coyotes. I feel sorry for Buck. He must be relieved that Snarl is defeated. I'm sure he's excited about Jennifer, but he won't be able to lead a pack of coyotes. The threat from the coyotes will disappear as they consume themselves with infighting once again. I just want to get away from Snarl's nasty carcass on my driveway. I can't wait until my people get rid of it.

After Buck leaves, I call to Max.

"It's time I address my subjects on this momentous day." I go back into the garage and find my cape. Max lifts me into the wagon. Max presses the garage door button a few times, and it opens. He pulls me in the wagon past Snarl. He takes me near the woodpile. I remember Snarl chasing me on this very path. I remember watching him leap over the fence and barely touch this woodpile. I climb the same woodpile with Max's help to address my domain.

Animals are making noise again. Birds chirp, bunnies hop, and even the skunk scurries about in the open. Everybody has a liveliness that I only see from children on Christmas morning. Best of all, I look over to Chief, and he's yipping like a puppy. No red threads are in sight now.

"Snarl is defeated," I declare. "He is done forever. He will never again frighten or threaten to destroy your life and family.

This is a new era in my domain. Some of you buckled under Snarl's oppressive and fear mongering threats. You gave way to temptation, and you hung a red thread on your door. You believed the lies that it would make you safe. You know it is not true, and Snarl is a liar." I give a wink to Tweedledee and Tweedledum; whatever their original motivations, they used the red thread for good when they delayed Snarl with the same string gimmick they embarrassed both me and Max with before.

"As your queen—nay, as your *empress*—I have proven my worthiness as your ruler by defeating the wicked Snarl. I grant all those who hung red threads amnesty. You will be treated as the most vocal supporters such as Chief, the bunnies, and Max. However, let it be a warning to you that you should never give in to fear, and never doubt Princess, the Empress of Rover Boulevard, Slayer of Snarl the Wicked Coyote."

Max carries me down to the wagon on his back. Max starts pulling the red wagon. This time, cheers rise from my subjects, and flowers are tossed at me. Right now, I look forward to laying in my favorite sunbeam in my house.

I'm doing just that several minutes later when I hear my people talking about Snarl. I reconstruct what happened after I came inside by listening to the big man person tell the rest of his family. The big man person had gone out to retrieve the Sunday newspaper from the driveway, and was disgusted to find an unconscious coyote lying there with a smashed skull. I think he figured it was the garage door that did it, but he has no idea exactly how it happened. The big man person called Animal Control to get rid of Snarl's body.

The big man person also said that the coyote (Snarl, he meant) was not dead.

That got my attention.

He was unconscious and badly injured. Animal Control said the coyote might live. However, he will not be able to live in the wild because of his massive head injuries. He will have to live in a zoo several hours away.

I have to admit, I wasn't sure I was going to be able to defeat Snarl. Before my people take me to the vet to heal my legs, I need to celebrate. Laying in my favorite sunbeam at the head of my people's bed, I decide I will even let Max join me. (As long as he doesn't play with my twitching tail.) Everything is calm and peaceful in my domain.

AUTHOR NOTES

Princess is the first cat I remember as a child, and we always seemed to have two cats. One was always older, and the boss.

Princess, like most cats, believed she was in charge, and she didn't like to be pet or cuddled. She really was a curmudgeon.

Max really was a bit of a goofball and a softy. He truly did try to convince birds to come down to him by meowing at them.

Princess and Max were accurately depicted; their personalities were distinct. Those who knew them would agree. They have both since passed from this world and can't sue me for libel.

The people in the story are, of course, caricatures. I wouldn't say they are even broadly representative of my parents and sisters. The depiction of myself as the middle boy child is probably the closest to reality. If my family is offended by their depiction in the book, my apologies.

The other animals, especially Snarl, were not real, as far as I know. Chief is a stand in for our neighbor's dog who was a much younger and more active golden retriever. Those meddling twins, Tweedledee and Tweedledum, are completely made up. I'm sure some of our neighbors had cats, but they don't stand for any specifically in my memory.

The setting is intentionally vague. It could be Anywhere, USA. I'm not sure where Princess will end up in all of her future adventures, and so I didn't want to limit her adventures unnecessarily. However, the presence of a rattlesnake and the mention of jackalopes should give you a hint.

So how did I even think of telling stories from Princess' perspective? My own kids recently reached the age when they could listen to me read chapter books to them. This was a huge revelation to me. Every parent is tired of reading the same memorized board books to their toddler, gutting through it because you know you should encourage reading. It's like magic when children become interested in chapter books because I like those books too. I remember reading them when I was younger.

My kids were especially enchanted by books with animals. Most animals die in such books (e.g.: *Where the Red Fern Grows,* and *Old Yeller*). They begged me to search for more books with animals - *that don't die*. So that's one ingredient: I knew kids loved chapter books with animals.

Second ingredient: What are the most popular Youtube videos? I don't know if this is actually true, but the popularity of silly cat videos is legendary.

Lastly, I grew up with cats with distinct personalities. I often told my friends at school about their antics.

Mix those three ingredients together, and what you get is the *Princess the Cat* series. As of this writing, there are two more in production.

If you liked reading Princess' adventure,sign up for the Princess the Cat Reader Group at: http://eepurl.com/crfeJ9.

You'll immediately get a free prequel short story.

Interested in receiving future Advanced Reader Copies (ARCs)? Email me at: john@flannelandflashlight.com.

Until next time,
    John Heaton
    December, 2016

Join the *Princess the Cat* Reader Group for a
FREE book.
Only fans like you will discover Princess' full story.

Join Now at:
http://eepurl.com/crfeJ9

Princess the Cat

ORIGINS

A Prequel Short Story by John Heaton

ALSO BY JOHN HEATON

Book Two

Book Three

Save 20%

Buy the digital Coloring Book with promo code **twentyoff** at:

https://gum.co/PtC01

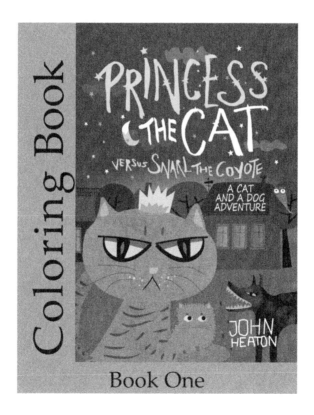

Printed in Great Britain
by Amazon

50885785R00092